DOCTOR ROSS OF HARTON

Esmond Ross was a widower. He ran his house and practice with the ordered routine of a gentleman's club with very little time for women, especially women doctors. When his new assistant arrived he was appalled to find that "Frankie" Cunningham was in fact "Francesca", young, attractive and wearing a black ski suit that was most unsuitable for a doctor's private practice. Francesca, immediately attracted by the taciturn Dr. Ross, found she had to prove herself as a doctor as well as a woman.

*Books by Alice Dwyer-Joyce in the
Ulverscroft Large Print Series:*

ALICE DWYER-JOYCE

DOCTOR ROSS OF HARTON

Complete and Unabridged

c.1

ULVERSCROFT
Leicester

Originally published in Great Britain in 1966 by
Robert Hale Ltd.
London

First Large Print Edition
published March 1983
by arrangement with
Robert Hale Ltd.
London

British Library CIP Data

Dwyer-Joyce, Alice
    Doctor Ross of Harton.— Large print ed.
(Ulverscroft large print series: romance)
I. Title
813'.54[F]   PS3554.W9

ISBN 0-7089-0927-2

Published by
F. A. Thorpe (Publishing) Ltd.
Anstey, Leicestershire
Printed and Bound in Great Britain by
T. J. Press (Padstow) Ltd., Padstow, Cornwall

TO
ANNETTE
AND
ROBIN

THE CHARACTERS
IN THIS BOOK

Esmond Alexander Ross, M.D., of Regent House, Harton.

Patricia Ross, his daughter.

Dr. Francesca Cunningham, his assistant.

Connie, his housekeeper.

Nurse Frances Roberts, Queen's Institute of District Nurses, later receptionist to the practice.

Simon, a Siamese gentleman of distinction.

Dr. Murdo Cunningham of Oxford, Guardian of Dr. Cunningham.

On the staff of the United Wentbridge Hospitals

Dr. Donald Evans Jones, consulting physician.

Dr. William Monaghan, consulting psychiatrist.

Mr. Oswald Caston Price, consulting obstetrician.

Dr. Alex Brough, house physician to Dr. Evan Jones.

The Wentbridgeshire
Constabulary

Inspector Percy Taylor, at Headquarters.

Sergeant Robert Bullen, at Harton Police Station.

Constable Hacker, at Headquarters.

Constable Tanner, at Harton Police Station.

and

the patients of the practice at Harton, who are the same as all patients, from Land's End to John o' Groats.

Love is
a time of enchantment:
in it all days are fair and all fields
green. Youth is blest by it,
old age made benign: the eyes of love see
roses blooming in December,
and sunshine through rain. Verily
is the time of true-love
a time of enchantment—and
Oh! how eager is woman
to be bewitched!

DOCTOR ROSS OF HARTON

ESMOND ROSS parked his car neatly between two others in the narrow side street. As usual in Wentbridge, it had been difficult to find a space and he had not felt up to the walk from the Multi-car Park. As it was, it must be a good two hundred yards through the frosty fog to Don Jones's consulting rooms.

"I shouldn't be too long, Simon," he told the Siamese cat, that sat on a blue cushion on the passenger's seat at his side.

He knew that his housekeeper would have put a hot water bottle under the cushion, as she never failed to do on a cold day and he smiled as he tucked the blue knitted shawl more comfortably about the cat.

Simon had had no objection to being kept indoors for the past three weeks. He had sat by the bedroom fire on the white fur rug, or stretched himself out on the eiderdown into what Connie called "a yard of cat." He hated the cold weather and had not really relished

1

the thought of the car ride today, but he always went everywhere with his master and he was not going to be left behind, just for the sake of a little personal discomfort. He watched Esmond lean over to get the walking stick from the rear seat and then he curled himself more tightly into a ball and prepared to wait.

"We'll go straight home afterwards," Esmond promised him and banged the door shut.

It was a bitterly cold day with the fog thickening as he came near the river. Don would grumble at him for venturing out, but he could not lie off work for ever. It had started after he drove to St. Catherine's to fetch Patricia home for the Christmas holidays. Poor child! She had not had much festivity this year, not that they ever indulged much in frivolity and amusement. He was always far too busy, though he did his best. It had been no fun trying to bring up an only daughter, since his wife had died after the child's birth. It seemed a hundred years ago now, he thought with a sigh, and got a vivid picture of the coffin being taken up the stairs the day it had come home from the hospital. He shuddered and thrust the thought back

2

into some sealed compartment of his mind.

He was very breathless today. Here he was not half way to Jones's rooms and breathing as if he had sprinted a hundred yards. Monaghan, the psychiatrist from the General, materialised out of the fog.

"Hello there, Ross! Glad to see you up and about again, but surely you'd be better off by your fire on a day the like of this?"

Monaghan still had that suggestion of Irish brogue, which put a smile into his voice.

"I want to get back into harness tomorrow and Don Jones won't hear of it, till he's screened my chest."

"Well, you don't look as if you should be at work, not by a long shot, but then I'm no chest physician and thank God I'm not. Why don't you cut and run . . . go off to the Bahamas like old Henderson did on his National Health award? He blued the lot, or so they tell me, and then the Income Tax demand arrived. Give with one hand and take away with the other . . . that's the Government all over, and it landed old Henderson up the creek. Still, you can't be financially embarrassed out at Harton, with all the building they're doing. They're making you quite a garden suburb, aren't they?"

It was frightening, Esmond thought, the way the new houses were mushrooming up in the village. The work of the practice had increased two-fold since his father's day and he was never done with it, and the patients had grown more and more demanding or so it seemed. He stopped at the window of an antique shop to get his breath and looked at his reflection in the wall mirror at the back of the displayed furniture. Monaghan was right. If a patient had looked like that, there would have been no question of work for weeks to come. He was too pale and his face looked lined and despondent. The white wings at his temples were fluffed out and far too long. He raised his rather Satanic eyebrows and wished he was back in his bed at Regent House, with Connie, his housekeeper, to fuss over him.

After a while, he was breathing more easily, though the fog was burning his chest. He walked on along the damp grey pavement and soon he had mounted the four steps and was pressing his finger against the bell under the plate marked Donald Evan Jones, M.D. He coughed a little and felt the sweat cold on his brow, knowing he had been a fool to attempt the visit.

"Good afternoon, Dr. Ross. Won't you

4

please come in? What an awful day!"

The receptionist showed him through to the big old-fashioned sitting-room, told him that Dr. Jones would be with him in a moment and closed the door softly behind her, as she withdrew. There was a painting of Mrs. Don over the mantelpiece and he stood before the fire and looked up at it. There had been a painting of Sheelagh, which had showed up all the golden beauty of her hair and the deep blue of her eyes. He did not know where it had gone to. Connie had taken it down after the funeral and he did not want to see it ever again. He had never spoken to Connie about it. Jones adored his wife. His study was full of photographs of her and the three children. A good wife and a happy home were the best possessions a man could have in life, but he would never be blessed with such happiness. It was all over and done with, and best forgotten. He sat down in a chair by the fire and thought that at least he had Patricia . . . and his household ran like clockwork with Connie in charge. You could not call it a happy home all the same, not like Don Jones had, with laughter and bickering in the nursery. Regent House had the atmosphere of a good men's club, luxurious, silent, efficient, nothing out of place, flowers perfectly arranged, his library book on the table by his armchair and Simon on the blue cushion by the fire.

"So here you are, Ross? I rang your house to put you off, but Connie told me you had just gone through the front gates. God! If you caught a post-pneumonia patient of yours out on a foggy January day like this, you'd skin him alive. Don't blame me, if you're in bed for another month after it. Did you get the car parked anywhere close?"

"Not too far away . . . a short walk."

"Well, come along then and we'll see what damage you've done. You're far too short of puff, you know, and you don't look well. I really can't see you going back to work yet a while, unless you want to kill yourself. . . ."

He led the way across the hall into the study he used for his consultations.

"Slip off your shirt and let's have a look at you."

It was strange to be on the receiving end for a change and Jones's hands were on the cool side, as he percussed the left base. It still sounded a bit dull, or so Esmond imagined. The cold tip of the stethoscope was a minor torture, as he breathed in and out obediently and said "ninety-nine," whispered "one, two, three."

Suppose he tells me I have an abscess or even a cancer of the bronchus? What then? Surely the breathlessness was not just post-pneumonic? He wondered if patients always felt as apprehensive as he did. Jones's face was so intent and grave, that he might be wondering how to break bad news to him.

"Seems perfectly clear, but we'd best have you behind the screen. I'll check your sinuses first of all, if you'll just slip out your dentures."

"My teeth are my own."

Jones grinned at him and told him he was a lucky man.

"At your age, that mostly means we've paid for 'em. They look far too perfect to be natural. No wonder you're such a handsome fellow. How have you managed it? Kept off sweets? The Public Health people have got a bee in their bonnets about that now, haven't they?"

"It's a matter of inheritance with me. My father still had most of his when he died."

The buzzing noise was loud in his ears and Jones's voice might have come from another planet.

7

"Now the chest. Just a few deep breaths. Yes . . . yes. . . . It seems to be all clear now and your heart shadow is O.K. just as a matter of interest."

Poor devil, Jones was thinking, everybody said that his heart was broken over his wife, but that was past history now. The daughter was the same age as his eldest girl . . . fifteen, that would be . . . pretty too, but not a patch on Sheelagh. Well, a broken heart did not show up on the screen, it seemed. Ross had not had any more to do with women all the same . . . never looked at them, or so people said, and he had not married again, even to get a mother for Pat. He was a fine-looking bloke too. A woman would love to look after him. Jones grinned to himself as he thought of the soft spot his own wife had for Esmond. "Her ideal man," she called him, when she wanted to tease. They dined out at Harton with Ross once or twice a year and the set-up out there was fantastic, with the whole outfit running on oiled wheels. That housekeeper of his was a treasure in this day and age. She had spoken to him on the phone just now and she sounded a bit like Monaghan, the psychiatrist, with her strong Irish brogue.

"Dr. Jones, will you for God's sake, do

something about Dr. Esmond? He's going to kill himself, if somebody doesn't put a stop to it. He's never done night or day with the way they're shoving up all the new houses. The patients are never out of the waiting-room, unless they're in their beds, sending for visits. He can't last out with the way it's been lately."

"And what would you suggest, Connie?"

"Make him take in an assistant, sir. He won't carry on another year, if he doesn't. I'm worried to death about it. Make him take on a younger man to help him. Wouldn't you have one of the junior doctors in the hospital, who'd take it on?"

"I'll issue the command this afternoon."

The brogue came out very strongly over the phone.

"And for God's sake, don't say it was me suggested it, sir. He'd eat me."

"Boiled or roast, Connie?"

"Go on out of that, Dr. Jones! You always have something funny to say. A person might be dying and you'd make a joke out of it."

"So all my patients die laughing then? That's a nice libellous statement to make."

He sat at his desk and looked across at Esmond Ross, with a sigh.

"Your lungs are clear, but you're an ill man still and well you know it. Your general condition is bad. Your haemoglobin reading is only 10.5. It's no good your expecting me to give you permission to go back to your twenty-four hour day, for I won't do it, but I'll solve your problem for you, if you like . . ."

Ross looked at him sombrely.

"A holiday is out of the question. I've told you that. For one thing, there are no locums. This lad I've got now is off tomorrow and there just isn't another to be had. God knows, I've tried."

Jones tilted his chair back and smiled.

"I didn't suggest a holiday. I want you to take an assistant."

"But——"

"There's no 'but' about it. Don't tell me you can't afford it. You can't *not* afford it, the way you are this afternoon. There are plenty of young chaps, fighting to get a toe in general practice in this area. I can give you my H.P. next week . . . Alex Brough. He's thrown up the idea of specialising now that he's got his eye on one of the staff nurses. He'd jump at the chance of getting married and settling down in Harton with you. If you don't want him, why not put an 'ad.' in the *Journal*? Do anything you like, but for Pete's sake, be guided by me."

He picked up a photograph of his wife from the desk.

"Why don't you get married again, for that matter?" he shot out suddenly. "You want a wife to see after you, as much as you want help in the practice. You're still a young man . . . early forties, like myself. Tell me to go to hell, if you like. I know I'm sticking my nose in, but it's for your own good."

He was startled by the bleak look that came into Ross's face, as the question took him off guard, and he regretted his impulsiveness. He would not have liked it much himself, come to that, if the positions had been reversed and Bunty were dead . . . even dead fifteen years. Ross had his face under control and was looking at him gravely, speaking in a low voice.

"I will never marry again. Besides, Patricia looks after me . . . and I have Connie."

"Pat and Connie can't get into your bed and lie in your arms and shut out the world . . . count the world well lost for you too, if it came to be lost."

He asked himself what sort of a fool he was

11

to say a thing like that to Ross. The man's face was a smiling mask, his eyes were like lead.

"I'll take an assistant. Will that content you?"

Ross stood up and walked across to the fireplace, leaning on his ebony stick, with the slight halt in his gait, that was so much a characteristic of his, and he kept his back carefully turned.

"I'd be obliged if you'd speak to Brough about it. He's a good chap . . . always most helpful. Perhaps he'd like to come out and dine with me one evening to talk it over. There'd be a view to a partnership of course, if we got on together. It's a dead end without that. He could live in till he wedded his staff nurse. Connie would love to have a young man to take under her wing."

The pretty young receptionist had come out of her office to show him to the door, but Jones waved her aside and walked out to the front steps to see him off.

"Driving will be impossible tonight. It's bad enough now. Watch how you go. It's always thick out in the Harton direction."

Ross walked back along the narrow street and stopped at the wine shop to order a case

12

of whisky to be sent to Jones in a day or so. He took out a visiting card and under his name he wrote "Thank you for your invaluable help." He had been going to add "And advice" and stopped up short. That advice about remarriage was sheer foolishness. It was just because Bunty was such a charming woman that Jones thought that all men must rush into wedlock . . . thought marriage synonymous with paradise, never realising that it might not be the common lot of all men to find happiness with their wives. He wondered if Jones would remarry if Bunty died . . . try to recapture the dream again. A doctor saw plenty of unhappiness in marriage. Happiness was a jewel of great price and the hardest of all jewels to possess. . . .

There were two girls by his parked car, for as usual Simon had found himself admirers. He was standing absurdly on his hind legs with his nose pressed to the glass of the window and the two girls were chattering in some foreign tongue.

"*Ach! Er ist schön! Das kleine Katzchen!*"

They were German au pair students over in England to learn the language and they started a little, as he got out the key to open the door.

"Are you making friends with Simon?" he smiled.

"He is so beautiful. Never did I such a cat see. Is it not too cold? Is he going about in the car every day?"

He saw the perfection of their young faces . . . the bloom of youth, which could never be recaptured, when lost, though "my lady paint an inch thick." He got into the car and settled Simon back on his cushion, showed them the hot water bottle.

"He's a very spoilt young gentleman. See?"

He smiled at their friendliness and thought how if fate had been kinder, he might have filled Regent House with such daughters. As he started the car and drove off in the direction of Harton, he wondered if that was the type of bride Don Jones wanted him to take to his bed. He pictured what it would be like to have one of them ruling his household and sighed at the imagined disorganisation. It would be strange to have bath salts in the bathroom again and powder on the dressing-table. His mind shrieked away from the vision of Sheelagh's great cut-glass powder bowl, that had caught and reflected the light rays like a diamond. Why could he not get her out of his mind today? Sometimes, he forgot her for weeks on end. To break his chain of thought, he stopped the car at a shop on the Harton Road and bought Patricia a box of her favourite chocolates. She had had a miserable Christmas. It was a good thing she was horse-mad at the moment and had spent every afternoon out riding with young Mallory, though Mallory was a flirt. He felt slightly uneasy at the difference of his daughter in boots and breeches and a hacking jacket to the picture she presented in her gym tunic. She had a look about her, that recalled Sheelagh. There he was, thinking about her again. Patricia had seen far too much of young Mallory, while he had been ill, but surely the chap would respect the fact that she was only a child?

He drove the car along in low gear, for the fog had thickened so much that he had to strain his eyes to see ten yards ahead of him. It stung his throat and burnt his chest. He had been a fool to leave his house on such a day and he knew he would cough all night. He got behind another car at last and as his vision closed down to ten feet, he hung grimly to its tail and relaxed slightly. Yet it seemed hours before they passed the thirty mile limit outside Harton. Another slow five minutes and they were turning into the High Street, two hundred yards from his gate. He was amazed to see the other car turn into the drive in front of him. He swung in behind it and saw it was an old Sports Bentley. A man had jumped out of it and had come to the car window.

"Blast you, Ross, dogging my rear lights like that! You nearly blinded me with those expensive foglamps of yours. Why couldn't you take the lead and done with it?"

The man was unwinding yards of thick knitted scarf from about his neck.

"Murdo Cunningham!"

"Aye it's me, right enough. I was over to read a paper at your blasted Symposium last night and this fog blew up, so I'm stranded. I hadn't seen you for a long time, so I thought I'd away over to Harton and beg a bed for the night . . . and a dram with an old friend. There's no chance of my getting to Oxford in this . . . not the foggiest chance."

He roared with laughter, as Esmond got rather stiffly out of the car and told him that his humour had not improved to any appreciable extent.

16

"Still, it's marvellous to see you. Come along in."

The front door had opened and a dark plump woman had come out into the drive. She collected Simon under one arm and picked up the hot water bottle in her free hand, scolding her employer as she did so.

"Will you come in out of that, sir? You'll catch your death out here . . . and is that you, Dr. Cunningham? You're welcome, I'm sure, for the doctor has been at death's door with pneumonia and he won't listen to any of us. . . ."

She shooed the two men in front of her into the square hall and the warmth of the house enfolded them in its comfort.

"Wouldn't it freeze the crows tonight? There now, Master Simon! Off in to the fire with you. You'll find your liver on the hearth rug."

She took their coats and hung them on the hall-stand, smiling all over her cheerful face, still chattering away in her soft lilting voice.

"I'll put the hot jar in your bed this minute, Dr. Cunningham. Isn't it God's blessing that you're here, for perhaps you'll cheer himself up. He's got so run down that I don't know what to do. Perhaps you can

17

make him see sense and take things a bit easier."

She fussed about Esmond as solicitous as a hen with one chick.

"Go on into the warm room now, sir, and I'll bring in the tray of drinks for you. . . ."

Murdo Cunningham sat down in one of the deep armchairs and stretched his legs towards the blaze, as he thoughtfully regarded the Siamese cat eating its supper.

"So that's what she meant when she said the animal's liver was on the hearth? I feared it was something far worse. We Gaelic races have a strange turn of speech an odd while, but it rings welcome in the land of the Sassenach. . . ."

Half an hour later, he was in possession of all the recent news of Regent House. The men were friends from their university days, though they had never kept in close contact, just drifting into each other's lives and out again. Murdo Cunningham was doing research at Oxford and he lived there with a niece of his, who was also his ward. Esmond had never met her, for she had always been at school or college, on his rare visits to Oxford. He knew that her parents were both dead and that Murdo had brought her up. It had been a kind of link that both men had had girls to bring up, with no wife at their side. Esmond had often wondered if the ward had caused Cunningham as much worry as Patricia caused him.

She came into the room as he thought of her and ran to the visitor's chair to throw her arms about his neck.

"Connie told me you were here, Uncle Murdo. Isn't it marvellous? I hope it stays foggy for weeks and you'll have to make it a long visit."

"My word, Mistress Patricia! You're growing up to be a bonnie lassie. You might be your poor mother all over again, if you weren't so like this old rascal here. You've not been out riding in this weather, have you?"

She had gone over to sit on the hearthrug at her father's feet.

"We were mucking out."

Esmond frowned down at her fair head and his voice was irritable.

"That expression always strikes me as being unnecessarily crude . . . and really, my dear child, you couldn't smell more like a horse than you do, if you actually were one. Please to go and have a hot bath and change into one of your pretty dresses for dinner, for

19

you'll have to help me to entertain our guest."

"Must I change, daddy?"

"You certainly must."

"May I wait till after tea?"

"We may not want any tea. Connie's sending in drinks."

"Connie's not to bring the drinks till we've had tea," the girl said sulkily. "I'm to pour out."

"Well, you'd better get out of that kit before you play hostess. The whole room stinks of the stables."

Cunningham noticed the droop of the young shoulders and felt pity in his heart for the child.

"Leave her alone, man. She's very bonnie as she is and I won't hear one word against her. Come over here to me, Mistress Pat, and tell me how you like that school of yours."

She went over to his chair by the simple method of crawling on her hands and knees across the rug to settle herself at his feet.

"You ken my girlie, Francesca, was at yon academy, so I'm quite familiar with it. She always said there were over many rules there, but I suppose you must lay down the law to the lassies. With lads, you can get out the birch rod. My lassie always said it was a fine penny here and a penny there and a hundred lines of Latin to write out, if you as much as blinked an eyelid. She held that she'd sooner have had the birch rod and done with it. . . ."

Connie came wheeling the trolley into the room with the tea things and she frowned as she heard Esmond ask his daughter if she had washed her hands. Why had he to come out with such a question, when Miss Pat was trying to play at being grown up?

"Of course, she's washed her hands," she said reprovingly and he saw his error and smiled slightly, thinking that Connie always stuck up for the child.

"How many lumps do you take, Uncle Murdo?"

"Seven."

He grinned across the room at her out of his bearded face.

"Seven?" she echoed in amazement and then remembered her manners and smiled at her father.

"You don't take sugar, Daddy?" she said formally and he raised his brows at her irritably.

"You know very well that I do not."

She flushed slightly and bent her head and

Cunningham felt angry with his friend, because he did not seem to have the imagination to realise how sensitive the girl was.

"Would you like some bread and butter, Uncle? Connie's crab apple jelly is marvellous."

Cunningham thought that she looked completely adult in her riding kit, yet her youth and her insecurity were revealed in the telltale pink of her cheeks and the droop of the fair head on the long graceful neck.

"Have you heard that your father is to take in an assistant?"

As he spoke the words, the idea came to him.

"You know, Ross, my boy, I've got the very person for you. I could have an assistant here in three days, who'd suit you down to the ground. I could give you a guarantee of satisfaction."

He put the small slice of bread and jam into his mouth and went on in a muffled voice.

"I happen to know of somebody, who is on the look-out for a job . . . could come at short notice too, or *would* do it, to oblige me . . . damned sound doctor . . . winter-sporting in Switzerland at the moment. You'd not get the equal of Frankie anywhere. M.R.C.O.G., Diploma in Child Health . . . house jobs here and there . . . registrar here in Maternity for a year."

"I've half promised the job to young Brough. He's Don Jones's house physician. . . ."

"Actually, it would be a bit of a favour to me, if you took this . . . this . . . this Frankie," Cunningham said and passed his empty cup to his hostess.

"Seven lumps in this too?" she smiled at him.

"Take a keek in the bottom of the cup," he told her in a serious voice. "If there's a wee bit sugar sticking in the bottom, make it six. Otherwise, the mixture as before, if you please, and I'll take one of Mistress Constance's hot scones."

He piled crab apple jelly on the scone and avoided his friend's eye.

"I promised . . . Frankie, I'd look out for a place. Then I forgot all about it, till you said you wanted somebody, but don't put yourself out on my behalf."

"Of course, I'd take any doctor on your recommendation, Cunningham. I know you wouldn't let me down."

Do you, b'Jove, thought his friend.

"I suppose I'd better telephone Don Jones and say the post is filled then," Esmond said. "We'll say it has been given to this Dr. Frank What's-his-name. . . ."

"Perhaps you'd better hear some more. . . ."

"Good Lord, Cunningham! Look at those degrees. The man's better qualified than I am myself. How old is he?"

"Twenty-five . . . twenty-six . . . thereabouts."

"It sounds eminently suitable. I'd be obliged if you'd get a cable off as soon as may be. What's the chap's name?"

Cunningham put the entire scone into his mouth and answered in rather a strangled voice.

"Same as mine actually . . . Cunningham."

He turned to Pat and smiled as he told her if she had been the mistress of the castle for three and twenty years, she could not have presided over the tea table more graciously and Esmond was murmuring almost to himself.

"Frank Cunningham . . . Frank Cunningham. It sounds very familiar somehow. Have I met him somewhere before, I wonder."

The bearded man got to his feet with a sigh.

"You have never met. That I do know. If you'll excuse me, I'll away and get that cable off. . . ."

He stood at the desk in Esmond's surgery and grinned at Connie as he lifted the phone to dictate the cable to his namesake in the distant Swiss hotel.

"The Message is . . . JOB AS ASSISTANT TO ESMOND ROSS, HARTON, OPEN TO YOU. WIRE TIME AND DATE OF ARRIVAL IF ACCEPTABLE AND PLEASE TO ACCEPT IT, MISTRESS FRANKIE. IT IS URGENT. HE IS ILL. LOVE. MURDO."

"Did the doctor agree to Miss Francesca coming?" Connie asked him in a surprised voice, as he replaced the receiver.

"He agreed to a Dr. Frankie Cunningham coming. That's the same thing, but he doesn't know it yet. I have an idea in my head that maybe he is under the delusion that he's engaging a gentleman."

"But you can't do that. Oh, God, sir, he'll never let her stay. He hates lady doctors and he'll murder us all when he finds out. Who'll dare to tell him?"

25

Cunningham stood up from the desk and put an arm round her shoulders.

"With luck, she'll tell him herself when she replies to that cable . . . and when she comes, teach her how to make that crab apple jelly of yours. I haven't tasted the like of it since I was a bairn in my mother's house. You cook as well as any good Scots lassie, Mistress Constance."

Connie was not to be deflected from her subject by soft talk. Her eyes were accusing as she looked up at him.

"But you made out it was a man, sir, and that was a wicked thing to do."

"I didn't say male and I didn't say female. I said neither one way or the other. He drew his own conclusions and who was I to argue with a sick man? Why should the title of doctor mean a male of the species? Tell me that. There are plenty of lassies in medicine that are the worth of two of the laddies and Mistress Francesca is a gey good doctor. Besides I did it for Pat as well as everything else. What's wrong with him, Connie? Is it because she bears a look of her mother? There's no love lost between them and there's overmuch coolness on his side. Poor bairn! She has both hands stretched out to him for affection and he doesn't even see it. You watch my lassie put that situation to rights, but never mind that now. I'll away in and tell him the cable's on its way, and then I'll put him into his bed, for he's a sick man."

Connie stood with her back to the door and barred his way.

"He's likely to be far sicker, when he hears what you've done. He won't go back on his word and he'll let her stay for a bit, but may God have mercy on her! The snubs he dishes out to his daughter are nothing to what the poor lady doctor will get. . . ."

"I doubt it," he smiled. "You don't know Francesca Cunningham. She'd be able for six like himself outside at the fire. Poor chap! He doesn't know what's going to happen to him. Ah, Mistress Constance, wait till you see my ward and the light of my life. I've brought her up the way few lassies have been brought up and she'll be a match for his silent dignity and his elegance and his Siamese cat. Lord love you, she's even a match for me an odd time, though I'd not admit it to her. I have pity for him. God send that he hasn't the courage to shut the door in her face!"

He took one look at his host, when he

returned to the sitting-room and packed him off to bed.

"I'll stay over for a few days and see to the practice. Mistress Pat here will entertain me to a fine dinner and we'll send you up a plate of broth and the breast of that fine fowl Connie has in the oven . . . a slice of Dutch apple cake too, if she hasn't forgotten how I like it."

She had not forgotten Dr. Murdo's desire for a Dutch apple cake. He ate it later, looking down the table to where Pat sat in Esmond's chair in a silk dress and little flat shoes, with a ribbon threaded through her hair that made her look like Alice in Wonderland. Cunningham thought how vulnerable she was and his white teeth gleamed through his beard.

"Yon doctor," he began. "Yon doctor, who's coming as the new assistant. You'd best know it's not a laddie. It's my ward, Francesca. It's time she was settling down and finding a home for herself. She's too old to be foot-loose and fancy-free."

Pat's eyes blinked wide open with the surprise his words gave her.

"Your Francesca! Oh, no, it can't be. She can't come here. Daddy would be livid. He doesn't like lady doctors and he'll be furious. He's awful when he's cross. He's silent for days on end."

Murdo picked up the leg of the chicken from the dish and handed it to Simon, who had come down from Esmond's room in search of the delicious aroma from the kitchen.

"Simon isn't allowed to be fed in here. Daddy would be angry about that too."

"What the eye doesn't see, the heart doesn't grieve about, Simmy, but don't carry your spoils off upstairs. Just sit you down under the table and eat it in peace and stop making that awful swearing noise. It was the action of a friend to give you the thing and I'll not take it back from you now."

He shook his head at his hostess and smiled at her rueful face.

"Your father's too proud a man to do much in the situation I've created. He'll let his new assistant come. Then he's far too much of a gentleman to behave badly to her. He was cruelly hurt at one time and he's never gotten over it. Perhaps my lassie might be the one to heal his wounds. I've known stranger things to come about. Still, I'll take it kindly if you'll

29

give her a hand for the start, just to oblige me."

"I'll probably be gone back to St. Catherine's before she gets here. I'll be specially nice to her in the holidays, but I probably won't see her before Easter. I don't come home for half-term."

"Don't you now? It would be no surprise to me, if you were to come home this next half-term all the same. Your father will be wanting you to meet his new assistant and he'll have the time to fetch you, now that he has somebody to help with the practice. It used to worry him when he couldn't get over to see you."

"Did it really, Uncle Murdo? Did he say that to you?"

"Ach! He was always on about it," he lied to her. "She'll be wanting your help too, I'm thinking, if your father is put out with her for not being a man."

He smiled inwardly at the thought of his ward wanting help from anybody and he was still amused the next morning about the whole situation, when Connie came into the breakfast table with the answer to the cable in her hand and planked it down by his side.

"Now the fat's in the fire, sir. That just

came in over the telephone. Glory be to God, but who is going to take it upstairs to himself?"

Pat came to his side to look down at the message, written in Connie's neat hand:

DR. ROSS, HARTON, WENTBRIDGESHIRE, ENGLAND. VERY PLEASED ACCEPT YOUR OFFER OF ASSISTANTSHIP. WILL ARRIVE THURSDAY WENTBRIDGE. SEVEN TRAIN. FRANCESCA CUNNINGHAM.

Murdo Cunningham folded it up calmly and put it in his pocket.

"This porridge of yours is the best I've tasted south of the border, Mistress Constance. I suppose I couldn't interest you in a position in Oxford, looking after a poor lonely old bachelor, who hasn't a soul to care for him in the whole world. . . ."

He grinned up at her, his teeth gleaming in his black beard.

"Of course, I'd double any wages you're getting here."

Connie shook her head at him reproachfully.

"You ought to think shame on yourself for the trick you've played in this house. God

31

knows what himself will say when he claps eyes on that message. I wouldn't be in your shoes for all the tea in China. I'm going to lock myself in the kitchen, till it's all over. The young doctor is doing the surgery and then he'll be out on his rounds. You have the whole morning to talk Dr. Esmond round to your way of thinking, and you'll not come out of it the winner."

He'd not come out the loser, Murdo thought, as he went slowly out of the room and up the stairs a quarter of an hour later. There were too many important issues at stake. First of all, there was Mistress Pat, who was not getting a square deal out of life. There was Esmond Ross, whose life had come to an end fifteen years before. Then there was his bonnie Francesca, with the heart of a lion, who had discovered that she had no heart at all. She might find otherwise in Regent House, given a little time to get to know this serious, silent man. He found Esmond in the bathroom, clad in cream silk pyjamas, shaving at the wash-basin.

"I'm having an old-fashioned shave today, Cunningham. These electric gadgets never give one that clean, cool feel. Sit down on the chair and talk to me."

Cunningham lowered the lavatory seat and sat down comfortably and Esmond smiled at his reflection in the glass.

"Rather an unconventional position, my dear Murdo," he said as he drew the razor down to remove the last swathe of lather from his face. He bent his head to dash the water against his skin and reached for the towel.

"Good Lord! I must get my hair cut. I look like an infernal girl."

"That reminds me, there's an answer to the cable. You've got your new assistant, arriving at seven this Thursday. I'll hang on here till then."

He walked through to the bedroom under the archway and laid Connie's message on the dressing-table. Then he sat down on the stool and began to comb his beard with immense concentration. In a little while, Esmond's hand came into his line of vision, as it picked up the sheet of paper. He sensed the stiffening of the body and heard the word "Francesca" hiss through Esmond's teeth.

"These Continental officials are the devil with English names. You said 'Frank' . . ."

Cunningham put up a finger to pull down one of his own eyelids and he studied it closely in the mirror.

33

"No anaemia there, at any rate. Are you taking your iron tablets regularly, old man, for you're as bloodless, as if the vampires had been at you?"

"Of course."

"Frankie's never called anything but that. I don't know why. I suppose it suits her in a way, but the other suits her too. Francesca is a gracious name."

"But I thought——" started Esmond and then suddenly he spun on his heel and went off into the bathroom again, reappearing in half a minute with a flask of after-shaving lotion in his hand. He scowled at his friend's back, and his voice was high with exasperation.

"It's your ward, Francesca. I thought it was a man and you did nothing whatever to correct my impression. Good Lord! I can't do with a girl here. I didn't even like the idea of an assistant in the first place, but Jones talked me into it, but a girl! Good God above!"

His hands were shaking so much that he dropped the bottle and it fell with a crash into the tiled hearth.

"Oh, damn and blast it!"

He sat down abruptly on the edge of the bed, as if his legs had given way under him and put his head in his hands. Murdo Cunningham sauntered across to pick up the dressing-gown from a chair and put it round the other's shoulders and Esmond stood up again and shrugged himself into it, tightening the fringed silk sash with despair in his heart. He could never take a girl into the practice, he thought. There must be some way out of it, yet he must on no account hurt his friend's feelings. He owed Cunningham more than anybody would ever know. When Sheelagh had died, he had thrown up his work and come over to stay at Regent House for a month . . . spoken to him night after night, about things he had never thought to discuss with anybody. He got a vivid picture of himself, standing in this same room with Cunningham lecturing him.

"And what of the bairn?" he had said. "What of your wee daughter, who has none to look out for her, but her own father? What of all your patients? Aren't they your children too, in a sort of way? You owe them a responsibility for your dead father's sake. You must bury your golden-haired lady and pick up the threads of living again."

It had been good advice. He knew it now. The pain was gone, or almost gone. Sometimes, it returned in force, and very occasionally, even now, he dreamt that he was back in those awful days and woke in utter despair.

He rang the bell for Connie and stood there, looking down at the splintered glass on the rug.

Connie tapped at the door and came in with her face frightened and still he stood there, with his eyes on the floor.

"I'm sorry. I seem to have made an infernal mess of things. Could you bring a dust pan and brush, please?"

The whole room was full of the spicy smell of the lotion and Simon was prowling about, his tail still fluffed out with the fright he had had, when the flask had shattered on the hearth. Connie fetched a dust pan and knelt down to rattle the fragments together with the hand brush.

"Don't fret, sir. It won't do the slightest harm. This stuff is all spirit. It won't stain."

Esmond had gone back to sit on the bed and he looked down at Connie miserably.

"By the way, Connie, my new assistant will be Dr. Cunningham's niece. I've never met her, nor have you, I believe. She's coming on Thursday and I'll collect her at the station in

36

Wentbridge and bring her back here. Can you fix dinner a bit later that night? Eight o'clock, say? Dr. Cunningham will still be here and that will make four of us."

Cunningham had gone to the window to look out at a noisy motor-bike that went flashing past and his voice was casual.

"I must be away on Thursday after my tea. Frankie won't be wanting to see me. I'll hold down the practice till then and she'll take it over when she arrives. She's a good bairn and you'll like her. I never did meet a person who didn't take to her at once and she's a gey strong lassie . . . plenty of work in her."

Esmond groaned inwardly at the thought of the Amazon, who was on her way to clutter up his life and Connie's words did nothing to comfort him.

"Shall I make up the front spare room, sir? It has its own bathroom and she'd find that handy."

He sat up on the edge of the bed as if he had been stung.

"Of course, she won't live in. Find her lodgings in the village. There must be plenty of places. Fix up a bedroom and a sitting-room and full board. . . ."

"Perhaps it would be as well if she had her

37

meals here, sir," Connie suggested in a soft voice. "Dr. Murdo is anxious for her to learn how to make that jelly of mine . . . and do porridge properly and that sort of thing."

He frowned at her and answered very shortly that perhaps that might be best and Connie went on more cheerfully.

"I think Nurse Roberts would put her up. She was going to take in somebody when she retires and she'd like the lady doctor. It would keep her in the swim. She's not looking forward to being out of things. Besides Miss Francesca is nice. Dr. Murdo says so."

"I'm sure she is," Esmond replied with no visible expression of enthusiasm, but Connie had returned to her scrubbing of the rug and Murdo had gone back to sit at the dressing-table to admire his own reflection.

"You should grow a beard, Esmond, my boy. A bearded man is irresistible to the ladies."

"Blast the ladies!" Ross said and stood up once more tightening his sash about his waist viciously.

"See to Dr. Francesca's lodgings, Connie. Get her comfortable quarters. She'll want to study presumably. She seems to be a blue stocking by the way she's collected degrees."

"What *is* she like?" Connie asked Cunningham. "Dr. Ross will want to know what to look out for on the platform. That evening train is always packed. Is she pretty?"

Murdo smiled at himself in the mirror.

"Good Lord, no! Nobody would call old Frankie pretty. She's healthy looking. I'll say that for her, but she's a trifle mannish and she's a bright strong lassie. She's no beauty like Mrs. Ross was."

Why did he have to mention Sheelagh in such a casual way, Esmond wondered, as the other man went on.

"She's not in the same street as Sheelagh. You'd wonder by some of the tricks she gets up to, if she's a woman at all."

When Connie had taken herself off downstairs again. Cunningham stood at the window and looked at the cottages on the other side of the wide road.

"Her parents were killed outright in one of the London air raids. She was but ten at the time, poor chick, and they had left me as her guardian. I'd have taken her in any case. There was no other body close to her. Her father and I were brothers, only children . . . you ken that."

He paused for a long time and there was silence in the room, but at last he went on, his voice softer than ever Ross had heard it.

"If I live to be a hundred, I'll never forget the day she turned up at Oxford. She was ten at the time and straight from school . . . in her navy gaberdine coat and black school hat, with elastic under her chin. The ribbon was red and white like Pat's. She was like a small forsaken elf, with her eyes as green as the seas in the Hebrides on an April day. Her face was white and woebegone. Aye! There was no sparkle about her that day, though it came back in a year or two . . . it came back. She stood at the door of my study. There had been some slip-up in the day they were to send her. It was to be the day after the funeral, but they let her off the same day . . . and there was I, just home from London, sitting miserable as old Nick in the dark room . . . and in she creeps, like a wee mousie, for the janitor had let her in below. She stood there and made me a grand speech. She must have prepared it and had it off in her head. It was all about my kindness in taking her into my home and how she would never be done thanking me till the day she died. It was the word 'died' that did it, for she came to a full stop and gave a wee gulp. Then she tried to get a hold of herself, but she failed. I held out my arms to her, for I couldn't have spoken if I were to get a million golden guineas for it. She came across the room to my arms like a bonnie wee bird . . . straight to my heart."

"She was a lucky child to have such a home to come to," Esmond murmured, but Murdo might not have heard him for all the notice he took. He was back in the study at Oxford all those years ago.

"She's never left my heart since that day. I think an awful lot of her, you ken. She's a terrific lassie. She was subdued for a long time and crept round the flat like a wee ghost. I'd find her curled up in the window seat behind the curtains, reading a book and never turning a page. Perhaps I'd find her greeting the odd while, and I'd take her in my arms and greet with her. Her father and I had been like David and Jonathan. . . ."

He turned slowly round to look across the room at his friend and his eyes were sad.

"I don't know why I'm telling you all this. I haven't spoken of it before, nor thought much of it, come to that."

"It's very good of you to give me your confidence," Ross said gruffly. "It's no joke to rear a motherless girl. I've found that out to my cost."

"In a year or two, she was the old Frankie again. The light came back to her eyes. You'll see what I mean. The dimples began to wink in and out on her chin. She had the heart of a lion and the answer to any situation I ever put to her. It used to be grey, when the holidays were over and she had to go back to St. Catherine's. You'll know what I mean. You have it with Pat. The damned flat would be like a tomb, still is now, if she's not there. We'd count off the days on a calendar. Then one day, she'd be back again . . . flying across the room to me, like she did that first day. . . ."

He went into the bathroom and poured out a glass of water, sipped at it once and emptied it down the drain.

"We used to lead the high life in the school holidays. Out to dinner we'd go, or up to London for a gay time. We gave famous parties, mixing her friends with mine and you'd be surprised at the fun we had. I suppose my friends might be called stodgy, but hers were the reverse. I mind one day, her ladyship got into an argument with one of the finest Latin scholars in the world about a point of grammar . . . all very foolish, but her colleagues backed her up. Of course, he led them on, till we all got involved in the blasted thing. He was pulling their legs and pretending to make mistakes, but I laughed so much that day, I wouldn't have believed it possible. He sent her a wee bouquet of flowers the next morning with his card, and under it he had written *Vicisti* . . . *Thou hast conquered*. She was delighted with it, especially when she turned over the back of it and read 'Perhaps not the dead languages, but my poor self.' Ah! Those were the days! I see her far too seldom, though we correspond twice every week."

"I suppose she'll be getting married one of these days, Cunningham. Lady doctors usually get wed early on in their career."

The other man had come back to sit on the dressing-table stool, with his hands loosely clasped between his knees.

"She tells me she was vaccinated against it. Maybe she'll confide in you one of these days. It was when she was in Medical School. She took up with some young laddie and I think she cared a lot for him, though he wasn't fit to lick her feet. She found out that he had another woman in tow. She laughs about it now, but she doesn't think it funny. Watch her eyes if she tells you about it. She's never been able to take another laddie seriously and it's a pity, for she's got what Charles Dickens called 'a loving heart.' She may be nothing much to look at, Ross, not what you'd turn to stare at, with your sense of perfection, but don't forget she has a loving heart."

"I wonder what the village will make of her," Ross remarked. "A lady doctor is a rare genus on the Fens."

He stretched his arms above his head and sighed. "I must get dressed."

Cunningham walked across the room and turned back the bed covers.

"Away back to your couch of ease this minute. You were coughing half the night and if you recall it, I'm going to take over the practice till she comes. I haven't practiced much clinical medicine for twenty years, so 'twill be a change for me. Maybe I'll get the chance to do a little research into the National Health Scheme. As for your patients, they'll welcome any change from me by Thursday... even a woman doctor. I promise you that."

He lifted Simon from his place by the fire and set him on the eiderdown.

"Frankie says there's no such thing as a lady doctor. She says that no lady living would do the things a doctor has to do. She's about right, at that."

Esmond lay back on his pillows when his friend had gone, thinking what an infernal mess he had made of the whole affair. Here he was, stuck with a woman in the practice . . . and worse, she would have all her meals at his table. He would never be done with her, this great Amazon, with the hearty sense of what was funny. It was not to be borne. He was done with women for ever. He disliked women . . . not Connie, of course, or people like Don Jones's wife, Bunty, but women on the hunt for husbands. So many had been paraded under his nose in the last fourteen years. Cunningham meant well, and he wanted the job for the blasted girl, because he knew that Esmond would keep an eye on her. He was as tactful as a great blundering bull elephant, charging into a shop, full of small glass animals on glass shelves. Of course, the lady would be the same type. He could picture her. She would be a six-footer, if she was Cunningham's niece . . . and the man himself admitted she was no beauty. That meant she was pretty unsightly and her wit

45

was crude enough. "No lady would do the things a doctor had to do!" Good lord! She would trample about the house like a horse in a white coat, neighing with laughter at her own jokes, like her uncle always did. How old had he said she was? Twenty-five or six? If a woman doctor was not safely married by that ripe old age, there was something drastic wrong with her. At any rate, he would have Patricia as a buffer for the first few days. His heart sank like a plummet, as he realised that his daughter was due back in St. Catherine's on Thursday afternoon. Murdo was to drop her off. That was the last straw . . . he would dine alone with his new assistant on Thursday evening. There must be some way out of it. He would pretend to be ill. He would refuse to get out of bed. Then she would pursue him to his room . . . sit on the edge of the bed perhaps. . . .

There was a soft knock on the door and Connie put her head in to tell him that Nurse Roberts was on the phone and would like a word with him, if he felt up to it.

"She'll take Dr. Frankie too, sir, and welcome, so that's one weight off our minds. . . ."

The District Nurse's faint Welsh accent was more marked over the phone.

"Good morning, Dr. Ross. Isn't this good news now? You've got some sense in your head at last and taken in a lady to help you . . . and you'll find a girl is twice as hard a worker as a young man would be. She won't always be drinking in the 'Red Lion,' instead of doing her rounds."

"I must thank you for putting her up for us. It's most kind of you, nurse."

"I'll be glad to have her and she can have her own little flat, so she's got quiet to study. She's got some good degrees, your young lady, or so Connie tells me. . . ."

His eyebrows shot up. So he had got himself "a young lady?" He wondered what the village scandal-mongers would make of that.

"I'll give her breakfast in the mornings, but Connie says that you want her most particularly to have her other meals at Regent House. It's a kind thought of yours and it will make her feel at home straight away. Connie says you were worried in case she'd think of herself as a stranger . . . and being Dr. Cunningham's ward, you wanted her to feel she was welcome."

So Connie had said that, had she?

47

His voice sounded awkward in his own ears, as he issued the invitation, that had just entered his mind.

"I'd be awfully glad if you'd dine with us on Thursday night, Nurse Roberts. Miss Cunningham will be arriving at seven. Patricia and I haven't had the pleasure of your company this holidays with this wretched illness of mine. Of course, Patricia will be gone back to school, but it would be kind of you to come. Perhaps you'd like to drive into Wentbridge with me to meet the train?"

"Indeed, I would. That would give her a proper welcome."

He progressed from one awkward suggestion to the next, with his thoughts rushing about like rats caught in a trap.

"I'll discuss terms with you on the way in, but of course, anything you say will be suitable with me. . . ."

"There's no question of terms, sir. What trouble is it to me to give the girl a bed and a bite of breakfast? She'll be company for me and I'll be only too pleased to be helping you out. You've helped us all out in this village for the past sixteen years."

"We'll quarrel about that on the way to

Wentbridge shall we? I'll collect you at your house, well before seven. I don't know how to begin to say 'thank you.' Of course, I could have had a male assistant sleep in, but with a woman . . . Connie suggested she had the front spare room here, but it would not be quite the thing for her to sleep with me . . . I mean to sleep at Regent House. . . ."

He was getting more and more into a tangle, he thought ruefully and was glad when the nurse's voice interrupted him.

"Now, don't you worry about a thing. You'll find it will all work out for the best and she'll take all the work off your shoulders. If she's Dr. Cunningham's niece, she won't be one for gallivanting after men and painting her face."

He lay back on his pillows, when he put down the phone, turning his head sideways and shutting his eyes. He must think of some excuse to get rid of her in a month or two, without hurting her feelings. He would invent a relative . . . a cousin, perhaps, who had to be given the job. He had no intention of being tied to a woman for the rest of his life, even Cunningham's ward. Rather than that, he would retire. He had enough to live on, if he cut his standards. Connie and he would take a cottage on one of the Hebridean islands and catch lobsters for a hobby. He had taken Patricia to the Hebrides one holiday in May and the seas had been as green and sparkling as a woman's eyes. That was what Cunningham had said about. . . . Oh, to hell with it. . . .

He did not wake till Murdo tiptoed into the room at seven o'clock that evening.

"Good Lord! I can't have slept all day. I haven't slept properly for a month."

"Your mind's at rest, Esmond, my boy. That's all it is. You've decided to lay down the burden and your mind's at rest."

Dr. Ross's mind was certainly not at rest, as he put on his dark overcoat on Thursday evening and got into his car to collect his new assistant at Wentbridge station. A sad-eyed, sober Patricia, in school uniform had departed that afternoon with Murdo in the Sports Bentley. She had looked no more than eleven years old, when he had taken her in his arms and bent to kiss her cheek. He imagined that she was not far from tears, as she mumbled against his neck, that he was not to be cross with Francesca. Cunningham had overheard her and his white teeth had gleamed through the black beard.

"There's a list of the patients to be seen tomorrow, on the top of the surgery desk. Keep your distinguished nose out of the practice till you can walk upstairs without puffing like a grampus. Give the list to Frankie and tell her to get cracking on it. If she doesn't do as she's told, you can be as cross as you like. You have my full permission to lay her across your knee and spank her, if it becomes necessary."

That had been a hell of a parting shot, he thought, as Connie opened the door to put Simon upon his cushion in the back window of the car. In under an hour now, the wretched girl would be in Harton. Spank her indeed! Connie was scolding the cat, because he was refusing to settle down in an unaccustomed place.

"You stop swearing at me, Simon, this minute and do as you're bid. Nurse Roberts will be getting in further down the road. You'll find her sitting on top of you, if you insist on the front seat. Some cats would think themselves lucky if they had a hot jar and a cushion and a shawl knitted in blue to match their blue eyes. . . ."

He spent the journey to town in a long wrangle with the nurse about taking a reasonable fee for Francesca's board and lodging. He won the argument eventually, but he could see she was in a huff with him for insisting that she accept what she considered to be an enormous sum of money every month. She did not say a word as they got out at Wentbridge station and walked into the big draughty hall to get their platform tickets. He limped at her side, leaning more heavily than was usual on his ebony stick and stood back to let her pass in front of him on to the platform. Then she noticed his worried serious face and smiled up at him suddenly.

"She can't eat us, Dr. Ross . . . and it's not the end of the world either. Come into the Refreshment Room and have a good stiff drink. It will give you Dutch courage."

He watched her sip her glass of sherry a few minutes later and he raised a brow at her scornfully.

"You surely do not think that I'd be frightened of a girl in her twenties?" he demanded and she laughed at the false front he had adopted.

"I'm frightened of spiders . . . and mice too, for all that I'm a deal bigger than they are, and older too. It's no shame to be scared of a stranger coming into your life. If I admit the truth, I'm in a bit of a blue funk myself at this very moment. . . ."

She thought what a striking-looking man he was, as they came out on the platform again. The wings of hair at his temples were silvery in the bleak light from the lamps and his face looked pale and remote.

"Let's be honest," the nurse murmured. "We're both terrified out of our wits, by what's going to step off the next train . . . and we won't have long to wait, for here she is now."

They had stationed themselves by the ticket barrier and as the carriages flashed past them, Esmond glanced down at his chamois gloves and saw that there was a black soot mark across the back of one of them. He must get it off anyhow to shake this woman's hand and he anticipated a grip like a navvy, if she were on the train at all. There did not seem one person who remotely resembled her description. The platform was crowded with students and their girl-friends and with anxious-looking country men and women on their way home from London. They had all gone past and still there was no sign of her.

Esmond felt a flood of relief that perhaps she had not arrived and he would have another few hours respite before the peace of his house was shattered.

"She must have missed the train, Dr. Ross. Shall I ask when the next one is due in?"

A slim girl in a black ski suit had appeared in front of him.

"I think you must be Dr. Ross," she smiled, her dark short hair blowing round her face in the draught of the station, her teeth as white as ivory against the sunburn of her skin.

"I'm Francesca Cunningham. I believe you're expecting me. . . ."

He put out his hand automatically and felt the warm feel of wool, looked down at the blue and white mitt she wore, his face incredulous for a moment, before he brought it under control. Cunningham had been pulling his leg, of course. The girl was beautiful. Her eyes were very dark in the uncertain, watery light of the platform lamps. She had a small triangular face and dimples, that came and went beside her chin. The top of her head reached to his shoulder, or a bit more, and she was as slender as a lath.

"There's no luggage," she laughed. "I've

lost it all . . . every last bit of it this time, so it's a record. It's between here and Dover, but that's all I can tell you. Murdo knows I do it all the time, but it saves carrying it. There's always a bright side to everything."

She looked at him inquiringly.

"You *are* Dr. Ross, aren't you?"

He was still holding her hand and he dropped it, as if it had become red hot.

"Of course, I am. I'm being awfully stupid. I expected someone quite different. Your guardian led me astray for some peculiar reason of his own. You must be tired. We have the car outside and dinner should be waiting when we get home. Oh, yes, and I was to tell you that you are most specially welcome."

They passed through the ticket barrier and he bent his head to ask her if he should inquire about the lost luggage.

"I told them on the train. It's no good worrying about it. I'm not very suitably dressed for dinner though, am I?"

"It's only Nurse Roberts and you and I. Good Lord! Forgive me, Robbie. This is our District Nurse, with whom you are to lodge . . . to sleep and have your breakfast. You are to have lunch and dinner at Regent House with me."

He wondered suddenly why he was so glad to tell her that. He opened the door of the car for the nurse to get in beside the driver's seat, but she got into the rear seat.

"Dr. Frankie must sit by you. She'll want to take a good look at Wentbridge again."

He limped round the bonnet of the car to get in beside her and she thought that the halt in his gait was not an ungraceful thing. Murdo had always told her that it gave him an inferiority complex, but it fitted him perfectly. He was far more handsome than she had imagined. He was elegant. That had always been Murdo's word for him.

Simon left the back window and jumped up on the seat at her shoulder, putting his nose to her ear to whirr a greeting. She started a little and then laughed.

"Simon? I know all about you."

She picked him up and cuddled him in her arms, dropping her face to put her chin on top of his head.

"I know how sophisticated he is. He has special blue covers for his cushions and Connie knits shawls, just to match his eyes . . .

and he's a most vain cat in consequence. Aren't you, Simmy?"

She glanced sideways at Esmond as he started the car.

"You couldn't believe all the things I know about Regent House, Dr. Ross. Murdo was never done talking about his visits to Harton."

She held the cat up against her shoulder and he pushed a velvet nose against her cheek.

"I suppose I should apologise for not coming out to see you when I was at the Maternity Hospital. Come to that, it was remiss of me not to look you up when I was at College. Murdo was very angry with me about it. I did intend to come, but I put it off from one day to the next. I was a bit frightened of you, I expect, from all Murdo said about you."

"Frightened?" he asked in surprise.

"Well, Murdo did make you out to be a little terrifying . . . nothing horrible, rather the reverse . . . a perfectionist . . . very serious. I was afraid I might disappoint you, after the glowing accounts Murdo might have given. He does it to all his friends . . . and then their faces fall, when I walk in. I've got a complex about it."

"And what about your very learned don and his erudition? *Vicisti?* That was it, I believe?"

"Oh. Murdo is too bad. He tells that one to everybody."

She leaned forward to look up at the flood-lit beauty of Queen's College Chapel and sighed.

"Wentbridge is wonderful. Even in mid-winter, it doesn't lose its timeless quality."

As they turned on to the Market, she looked round at Nurse Roberts with the air of a conspirator.

"I know all about you, nurse. You taught Dr. Ross all the midwifery he knows and you're as staunch as the Rock of Ages, no matter how grave the emergency. You have a fine touch with fussy relatives too and keep them out of the physician's hair . . . and in addition, you're the best District Nurse in England, Ireland, Scotland or Wales."

Nurse Roberts was pleased with the compliment. It was obvious that Dr. Cunningham had told his ward all that nonsense and it was a nice feeling that Dr. Ross must have praised her like that. She had come to Harton, when he was still a school-boy in short pants and a blazer. She remembered how she used to make him a tin of home-made toffee at Christmas and on birthdays.

" 'Roberts' is a common name," she murmured. "I think you've got the wrong nurse. Dr. Esmond thought I was a right 'Sairey Gamp', when he came to the practice first and I'm afraid he's had no reason to change his opinion since."

"That's ridiculous," he objected in a serious voice. "You know that I never thought you old-fashioned, nor inefficient in any way. . . ."

He broke off then and added, "Oh, I see you're only jesting."

They had stopped at traffic lights and he glanced over his shoulder at the nurse and then looked sideways at Francesca.

"That picture was a very accurate one, Dr. er . . . Cunningham. It's a most able description of my colleague in the rear seat . . . most accurate, in every last detail."

"Nurses always get all the kicks and few of the ha'pence in the midwifery racket," Francesca remarked and then draped Simon 'round her neck like a fur collar.

"Ouch, Simmy! You're not going to knead dough on my shoulder, if you're going to stick your claws that far in . . ."

Nobody had ever thought to put the dignified Simon in such a position before and Esmond was surprised that he did not resent it. It was quite clear that even the cat had been won over by her charm. He wondered what she would look like in a strong light. Perhaps the station lamps had been too kind to her and she was not half so lovely as she had appeared on first sight. She certainly was not mannish . . . boyish perhaps, but a far cry from Murdo's picture of her.

"You've never been to Harton?" Nurse Roberts was asking and she shook her head.

"Only in my imagination . . . and in Murdo's letters and conversations. I have a very clear picture of it all the same. I know the house and Connie . . . or I think I do . . . the hall, the staircase, the big surgery at the back. It will be like reading a book after seeing the film. I expect I've got it all wrong, but I had you right, Nurse. . . ."

She did not tell Esmond how wrong had been her mental image of himself. Perhaps it was because Murdo was so very hairy about the face, that she had pictured him with a

bushy moustache and longish white hair. She
had thought of him as a tall, lanky, question-
mark-shaped man with glasses and rather a
cadaveric face. She had heard of the sartorial
perfection, of course, but she had written that
off as a navy-blue serge suit with a red
carnation in the button-hole. She had been
astounded to see the man, who was obviously
waiting for her on the platform, for of course,
that was Roberts in her Queen's Institute of
District Nurses uniform . . . but he was very
good-looking and very sophisticated too. The
silver flashes in his dark hair, the pale serious
intent face, even the halting gait and the
Siamese cat . . . it all added up to something
which attracted her at once. Murdo had given
her a false impression of him, or perhaps she
had made it up for herself. Murdo had told
her that he had great tufts of hair sticking out
of his eye-brows. She had visualised fierce
jutting brows and here she found him with
brows, just right for the rest of his make-up,
like devil's brows, she thought, slanting in a
most attractive way, with small tufts of hair,
where they curved upwards. He was talking
to the nurse about some patient, who was ill,
and Simon was purring in her ear, as the car
ran swiftly out along the flat fen road. She

61

regretted the loss of her baggage. It would have given her more confidence if she could have changed into a pretty dress . . . and here she was in a black ski suit and great thick boots. She had a powder compact, a lipstick, a comb, a handkerchief and money, in her pockets, but she had arrived at a crisis in her life, quite literally in the clothes she stood up in. His pleasant voice brought her back from her thoughts.

"This is the village now. They're all patients, of course, and you'll get to know them in time."

As soon as the words were out of his mouth, he wondered why he had said them. Surely he had been planning to get rid of her in a month or two?

"Regent House is just here on the left. . . ."

She laughed at that and he thought what a happy sound her laughter had.

"Dear me! I must have seen it all in the mirror. My Regent House was on the right."

Connie must have been on the look-out for them, for the door opened as the car turned into the drive and both lamps were lighting. Connie was on the front step, as they drew to a halt, looking to see what the new doctor was like. Francesca had jumped out of the car with the cat still draped about her neck like a very exotic collar and Simmy was beginning to get anxious about his new position and was wanting to get down, so the girl was finding herself in some difficulties. She stood in the light, which streamed out from the hall, laughing again.

"All right! All right! Master Simon! I'll lift you down if you just give me time. Come on round this way and keep on coming . . . and please to stop putting your spiked boots into my shoulder."

She arrived round the car bonnet bent double and straightened herself up in front of Connie, as the cat leapt to the ground. She put out a hand to shake the housekeeper's hand.

"You're not Connie?" she cried in an unbelieving voice. "My Connie is old. . . ."

She walked into the hall and stood looking all about her. Then she went into the sitting-room and the others followed her.

"It's far nicer than the book. It's not what I thought . . . not in the slightest. It's not old and dark and gloomy. It's a happy house. . . ."

Esmond got his first clear view of her, as she stood with her back to the fire and her hands clasped behind her back.

"Oh, Connie, do you know what my guardian says about you?"

The housekeeper thought suddenly what a foreign sound her laughter had in the gloomy dignified house and Nurse Roberts was smiling all over her face. The whole room seemed to be caught up in a web of joyousness, that Francesca cast about her.

"You're the best cook south of the border, Mistress Constance . . . and your scones must be eaten with guid Scots heather honey in the comb. . . ."

She was imitating her guardian's rich Scots accent in a shameful way and Ross's face was the only serious one in the room.

"Your porridge is the best outside the Highlands and the whole establishment runs like the works of a clock. If I were to drop my handkerchief on the floor this minute, I'd find it in a wee while, all freshly laundered and smelling faintly of lavender."

"That's very complimentary of Dr. Murdo. Was himself beyond in Ireland kissing the Blarney stone . . . or maybe, that it's you that went there, with all this soft talk of yours?"

Francesca frowned at her and made a self-deprecating face, shrugging her shoulders as she did so.

"Ach, there's more to come, Connie, but it's no' so guid as the first bit. He says that you set guard over the doctor . . . and that you're mighty fierce about it whiles . . . and that one day, you only just stopped short of boxing my poor guardian's ears. . . ."

"I'll box your ears for you my lady, if you don't stop inventing this nonsense to make us all laugh."

Esmond had gone across to the drinks cabinet and was offering her a glass of sherry.

"You must be very tired. Wouldn't you like to sit down?"

He was amazed to see her sit down on the floor beside Simon and lean back against the arm of the nurse's chair, more amazed to see Roberts's hand go out to tidy the dark, silky hair, as if she liked to touch it."

"Is my hair in an awful state, Nurse? I must tidy up before dinner."

Connie took her upstairs eventually and showed her into Patricia's room. Some of the girl's clothes would fit her and she could borrow anything she wanted till her own luggage was found.

". . . Although you look very nice in that

rig-out you've got on and it's like what a boy would wear, so the doctor won't grumble. He thought for a while that Dr. Frankie Cunningham was a gentleman, for Dr. Murdo made a right hare of him. It was an awful let-in, when he found out who was coming, for he doesn't hold with lady doctors. Still, he isn't the sort of man to hurt anybody's feelings, and it's all come right in the end, for nobody could help liking you once they'd clapped eyes on you."

She took the glass of sherry from his hand, when she went back to the sitting-room and went over to stand with her back to the fire once more. As he decanted the burgundy for dinner, Esmond took a good look at her. She had taken off her jacket and he saw the thick roll-necked sweater in a Fair Isle pattern of blue and white, that matched the blue eyelets in her ski boots. She was very slight and her breasts were as small as a young girl's. Her teeth were as white as milk against the dark tan of her face, and her lips were well-shaped and soft looking, her nose straight. There was a magnetism about her, that made him want to put out a hand to touch her hair, as Robbie had done, yet she was fidgeting a bit and he thought she looked nervous. She turned to put down the sherry glass on the mantelpiece and faced him again with her hands clasped behind her back in the pose, that seemed so characteristic of her. She was conscious of his scrutiny too, or so it seemed.

"Please don't say I won't do," she begged him. "I look frightfully efficient in a white coat, and when I put on a gown and mask, they tell me I'm like a real doctor. I don't look like this, when I'm dressed in a civilised fashion. I'm afraid I've given you a bad impression, arriving like this, but I only lose luggage, not important things."

"I should have thought luggage was an important thing," he said dryly, lifting a cynical eyebrow at her.

"I meant really important things, Dr. Ross, like lives and patients and swabs at operations . . . and one's nerve . . . one's temper . . . one's sense of proportion. . . ."

It came out in a rush like "cabbages and kings," but it was a clever speech for all its ingenue quality.

"Perhaps I should ask you if I would do," he said, in his serious pedantic way. "After all, there are two sides to every bargain."

The cat had climbed up to put his paws on her knee, to attract her attention and she bent her head down to talk to him, with her dark hair falling down to hide her face.

"I must confess I was doubtful when I got the cable," she said in a low voice. "My picture, my mirror image . . . the house on the right, as you come out from Wentbridge . . . was all rather a special sort of dream, and I might not have fitted into it."

She straightened up and came walking across the room towards him, her hands out by her side, turning about as she came.

"I like Regent House, and Connie and Nurse Roberts . . . and patients are patients, from Land's End to John o' Groats."

She came to a halt in front of him and he almost asked, "And me? Do you like me?" Then he wondered why he wanted so much to hear her say she liked him. What did it matter, one way or the other? The laughter had gone from her eyes and the light from her face.

"It's not any good really? Is it, Dr. Ross?"

"What do you mean?"

"I'm sorry about not being a male doctor. Connie told me about it upstairs just now. Murdo was quite wrong to have tricked you, like he did. It put you in an impossible position. I'll pack my bags and get out."

She smiled a small ghost of her former smile.

"That is, if my bags have turned up. I'll get out, as soon as you're better. I can see you're still quite ill, so please, don't worry about it tonight. I'll see to the practice, till we find somebody else to take over. There are plenty of people, who would sell their souls to come into a practice like this."

He got an idea that there were tears in the back of her voice, but she had spun away from him and had gone to the fire again, keeping her back turned, gripping the edge of the mantelshelf with both her hands.

"Murdo got some idea into his head. God knows what! You never know with Murdo, but it was foolishness. I apologise for what he did. We won't let him get away with it, all the same. I'll have seen Harton too, so I won't be dependent on my mirror image on the other side of the road. I assure you that this is a far pleasanter place. It's my idea of a real home . . . like Murdo's flat . . . a kind of safe place, where you're glad to find yourself, when you're lonely . . . and in terrible trouble. . . ."

She was back in the navy gaberdine coat and the black school hat with the elastic under her chin. Her parents had been killed three days before and she had been sent from boarding-school on the wrong day. He sensed it in a flash of intuition, the first of many to come. He was on a strange spiritual plane with this girl. He could not think of her as a woman. He knew with a great certainty that she had been very pleased to come to Murdo's friend. She had liked the place and then Connie had told her about what had happened. Connie was a fool, he thought angrily. She had felt again, in some infinitisimal way, that she had come, looking for a home . . . and then found that "she would not do." She was hurt by it . . . deeply and grievously hurt, yet she had a reserve about her. She was not the child she appeared to be on the surface. She had turned round once more and was smiling at him, pretending it was all an enormous joke. For a moment, he almost held out his arms to her, as Murdo had done . . . and then wondered what the devil had got into him. He walked quietly across the room and took her shoulders between his hands. She was as slender as Patricia, but she was vastly different in the effect she had upon his senses, for he experienced a most definite electric shock, that ran up his arms and gave him a strange ache in his chest. He told himself that it was a physiological thing of no importance and he gave her a small shake, as he might have done to Patricia.

"Don't disappoint us all. I was just thinking how well you're going to fit in. I know Nurse Roberts was of the same opinion. I was about to tell you that it's an assistantship with view to partnership, when you started off on that nonsense about packing your bags. I hope you won't leave Regent House for many years to come."

Now what on earth had made him say that, he asked himself. If he had only held his tongue, he could have got rid of her, but the sunshine was back in her face once more, as she looked up at him.

"So I can stay?" she asked him in a breathless little voice. "I can stay?"

"Of course, you can stay. I'll be very honoured to have you to help me."

The dining-room, with its oval, mahogany table and its Chippendale chairs, was a gracious room, Francesca thought. The light reflected from red-shaded candles to gleaming silver and glass, as she sat watching her new chief and thinking how apt had been

Murdo's description of him as "elegant". He looked far younger than her guardian, who was so different in every way . . . untidy, unkempt, unshorn . . . a strange person to bring up a child of ten years of age, and a girl at that. Yet there had been nothing but wisdom in his guardianship. He had given her an odd code of honour, but unfailingly, it worked. "Put yourself in the other fellow's shoes" had been the first commandment and there were a host of others, which included "Don't ever forget that God is a gentleman" and "Never be a sneak-thief or a tell-tale."

He had given her rough discipline and summary justice. As she drank her soup, she thought back to the day, when a son of a friend of his had come to tea . . . a boy of about eleven, the same age as herself. They had retired to her den and the boy had produced a packet of cigarettes, but she had refused to smoke in rather a prim, old-fashioned, self-righteous way. She had felt jealous of the professional manner in which he smoked his own cigarette, for she had never been able to manage the art without coughing. An hour or two later, they had had an argument, which childishly had led to blows and she had come off by far the worst.

At that point, she had decided that it was her bounden duty to report the cigarette-smoking incident to her uncle. She had marched along to his study with her friend mentally grovelling at her heels, and arrived there, she had revealed the horrible story. Murdo had regarded her for a minute without a word. Then he shrugged his shoulders.

"What punishment shall I give him, Mistress Cunningham?"

"I don't know."

"Oh, come now, lassie, you carried the tale. Don't put it on my shoulders. Shall we say twelve good slaps across the rear end . . . and done with it? That's what his papa gave him last week for the same heinous crime."

"Six would be enough, Murdo," she had answered primly.

"Six good slaps across the rear end . . . and that's your final decision. No tempering of justice with a bigger per cent of mercy?"

He was not pleased with her, for he scowled very blackly at her over the big desk.

"Not too hard, just to let him feel it's a wrong thing, when his father told him not to."

"Because his father told him not to?"

His voice had been incredulous, but she

had stuck doggedly to her false principle.

"His father doesn't like him to smoke. . . ."

"His father can bloody well lump it then," he had shot out. "Very well then, six medium hard slaps it shall be. Walk over here, laddie, and see justice done."

She remembered the ignomy of finding herself face-downwards across her guardian's knee.

"Carry nae mair tales tae me!"

He had underlined each word with a hard slap, his voice very broad Scots, as it always was in an emotional crisis. Worst of all, the boy had laughed at the discomfiture and she had felt burdened down by the shame of it.

"Aren't you going to beat him?" she had demanded furiously, when he let her up, but he had turned his back upon her.

"All gentlemen smoke."

The boy had laughed again at that and Murdo had swung round on him.

"What's so funny? I don't see anything to laugh at. She's twice the man you are, for you yelled like a stuck pig, when your pa whacked you last week and he hasn't half the strength in his arm that I have. My lassie isn't even greeting. She knows well that she deserves what she got and she won't sin that particular sin again, but she's got more courage in her little finger than you've got in your whole body. Away home with you now! It's time you were going anyway. . . ."

He had put his arm round her shoulders after the boy had gone and she had realised that he loved her no less than he had always done.

"If we were to bring a cushion for you to sit on, would you care to come to the pictures with me? There's a Mickey Mouse film on in your favourite cinema, that I'm longing to see . . . and perhaps you'd keep me company? There's no company in the whole wide world that I prefer to your own. . . ."

Esmond had gone to carve the chicken, when she brought her thoughts back to Regent House. He took his ebony stick, even to walk across the room, for he never went far without it. Murdo had told her it was an old Rugby injury and that he got pain from it sometimes even now. A fractured femur, that was it, that had happened at school.

Simon had trotted at his heels and was stretching his paws up towards the carving table appealingly, but Esmond glanced across at her.

"Don't give this chap any chicken, Dr.

Cunningham. It's a strict rule of the household that he is never fed at table."

Simon, like all clever cats, recognised the weakness of her resolution. He came to sit by her chair, his two eyes glowing like sapphires and she shook her head at him and bent to stroke him.

"You heard what King Cophetua decreed, Simmy," she whispered, wondering what had made her call him that, as if she fancied herself in the *rôle* of beggar-maid. Simon stood up on his hind legs and put a carefully sheathed brown paw on her knee. His purr vibrated through the quietness of the room and his eyes never left her face.

"Is there much midwifery, Dr. Ross?" she asked, as Esmond returned to his chair.

"About sixty cases a year. I run special ante-natal clinics."

Francesca moved a small piece of chicken over to the edge of her plate and then nodded her head at the oil painting over the fireplace.

"Is that a portrait of your father, sir?"

He glanced up at the picture and so did the nurse, and in a flash, the chicken scrap had been transferred to Simon, who went under the table with his prize. To Francesca's horror, he immediately set up a terrible growling sound, as he dared all comers to take it away.

"Yes, indeed. I took over from him soon after I qualified."

He stopped to look under the table and inquired rather testily what on earth was the matter with the cat. Francesca kept her eyes on her plate, and soon Simon had reappeared at her side, whirring like a small windmill.

"Is he being a nuisance? I'll ring for Connie and have him banished to the kitchen."

She met his eyes guilelessly down the length of the table.

"Of course not. He's only asking for some of my chicken in a perfectly gentlemanly and dignified way. Don't you think we might waive the rules for once and let him have some?"

He frowned at her.

"But it wouldn't be for once, doctor. You don't know Simon. We've made a most strict rule about it and you need have no pity for him. Connie overfeeds him as it is."

Simon's velvet nigger-brown paw touched the edge of her plate and she glanced up at the portrait once again.

"You're very like your father, Dr. Ross . . .

77

exactly the same eyebrows and mouth . . . something in the expression too."

He looked back again to the table in time to catch her in the act of transferring the morsel of chicken to Simon and thought irritably that it was just the childish sort of thing she would do. He considered her face in the candle glow, not smiling when she looked at him, wondering if he had seen her act of disobedience. Simon growled under the table for a moment and then he jumped lightly to her lap with a small grunt, put his two paws on her shoulders and rubbed his nose against hers.

"Simon! You're a betrayer of fair ladies!" Esmond scolded him. "For shame!"

He was smiling at her at last and asking her if she had not yet learned that some gentlemen were not to be trusted. As soon as the words were out of his mouth, he regretted them. He remembered her "vaccination against love." The sun was gone from her eyes, though she was smiling still, as she turned it off neatly.

"It wasn't a betrayal. He was just trying to make a rough estimate as to how much chicken I have left on my plate."

With the strange intuition Esmond had

about her, he knew that she had realised that Murdo had told him about the "vaccination" and that he was sorry he had spoken about betrayers. He felt closer, in some intangible mental way with this young woman, than ever he had felt with anybody before. He could not understand the pain he felt, that he might have caused her anguish by his careless words and he raised his glass and tried to make a reparation.

"A toast, Nurse Roberts! To Francesca, who will please regard Regent House as her home, where she is most cordially welcome."

The "Francesca" pleased her. She put down her head to the cat for a moment. Then she looked along the table at Esmond and smiled.

"Simon says I'm most welcome too, but his opinion is suspect. He's been accepting bribery in the form of baked meats. . . ."

She paused for a few seconds and then went on in a small, rather embarrassed voice.

"Thank you for saying that this is my home. I've only had that said to me once before, a long time ago, by the 'First Gentleman . . .' "

So that was what she called Murdo.

"He's an old friend of yours and he's

directly responsible for my present happy position in Harton. I'll try my hardest not to be too great an incubus in the practice. . . . I apologise too for not being the right sex, if you wanted the other. Gosh! There's a way to put it. The First Gentleman never did bring me up as a proper lady. . . ."

She had a girlish, untouched quality about her, he mused to himself, wondering what the patients would make of her. As it was, he had not to wait long to find out, for just as they were finishing the meal, Connie put her head round the door.

"There's an accident case in the waiting-room, sir . . . Nigel Thoms, brought down by his mother with a terrible cut on his leg. He fell through a glass window."

"Will you two ladies excuse me?"

"I think I must remind you that I'm on duty, Dr. Ross," Francesca said. "If Connie will show me where everything is. . . ."

It was a temptation to let her do it. He still felt far from well and he was curious to see her at work . . . see what she made of things.

"Come with me, then."

The surgery was a great old-fashioned room, thirty feet square, at the end of the hall, and Nurse Roberts carried in the screaming boy from the waiting-room, with the mother following at her heels.

"Would you like to sit at the desk and issue instructions, sir?" Francesca smiled, as she went by him to stand by the couch.

Nurse Roberts had busied herself putting the stitching kit in the steriliser.

"You're called 'Nigel' then? Let's look at this cut of yours. Hm! There's not much wrong here that we can't put right, you know . . . and there's no cause for tears. Sir Nigel was a very brave knight and he never cried like that, when he was a boy. You're called after him, I suppose?"

She was cleaning the wound in a very matter of fact way and the boy had stopped crying to hear what she was saying.

"I'm called after my Uncle Nigel," he volunteered.

"Well then, your Uncle Nigel would never had cried over a cut like this, would he?"

The child looked at her scornfully, his face dirty and tear-stained.

"You're wrong there, Nurse," he snuffled. "Uncle Nigel blared like a bull, every time he did anything to hisself, when he was my age. You ask my Mum. She says that he goes on the club now, do he have the finger ache."

Her eyes came across the room to Esmond, as if she invited him to share the humour of medicine with her.

"This is a lady doctor, Nigel," Nurse Roberts said stiffly. "You mustn't call her 'Nurse'."

"Is a lady doctor over a nurse?" the boy asked and Francesca shook her head gravely.

"Of course not, we're all a team. I'm just in a different part of the field. It's the same thing as if I'm wing and Nurse Roberts here is centre-half. We're both jolly glad to know that the other one's there . . . and we can rely on each other to see that the other side's kept out. . . ."

She drew up the local anaesthetic solution into the syringe and went on in a very casual voice.

"It's a tremendous team . . . nurses, doctors, chemists, surgeons, all sorts of people, even the people who made this stuff to take the pain away."

"Do you wear them trousers because you play on a team, miss?" the boy asked in the high treble of childhood, and again, she looked over at Esmond with a faint smile.

"Not really. I've just come home from

holidays. These were for skiing . . . on the snow you know."

She washed her hands for a long time at the basin and there was silence in the room, till the boy spoke again.

"It's like the Mounties on the telly. That's what it is. Do you go on the telly, miss?"

"Not yet, but I haven't given up hope."

"Do you go on them big jumps in the snow . . . down a slide, like in the pictures? Cor! It's wizard! They fall ass over tip, an odd time. . . ."

"*Moi aussi!*" she assured him in a serious voice. "That's French for 'Yes, in a kind of a way'."

"Perhaps it might be more literally translated as 'Me too'," Ross put in in his pedantic manner and she looked at him again and smiled. She had crossed to the couch and picked up the syringe, hoping that the child would not make a fuss. Her heart sank, when Esmond stood up from the desk and came across to watch her. She concentrated on the job in hand and saw his shoes come into her line of vision, as he leaned on his stick three feet away. The boy's voice broke hysterically as he asked what she was going to do. It would be the easiest thing in the world for him to relapse into struggling, fighting terror.

"I don't want any pricks," he cried and she looked at him calmly.

"If I'm going to hurt you, I'll tell you in advance. That's what we do in the . . . Royal Canadian Mounted Police. This is going to be like a cat scratch . . . a little sharp perhaps, but nothing to worry you."

"Are you in the Mounties?" Nigel asked her.

"I used to be, when I was your age."

"Did you go out on your skis in the snow, with them big dogs and all?"

"I expect so. Now, here's your scratch, but it's nothing the real Sir Nigel would have even felt, is it? Nurse has a sweet for you. That's a bullet to bite on. That's famous. You're doing very bravely, aren't you?"

She got the local in without any fuss and watched Nurse Roberts lift the instruments from the boiling water. She was very nervous, because Esmond was watching her and her hands were inclined to shake. If she was not careful, she might start to drop things, she knew, and decided to cut him out of her thoughts, but the patient defeated that notion at once.

84

"Are you Dr. Ross's wife?" he demanded and she shook her head.

"Why ain't you?"

"I took a vow of celibacy, when I joined the Mounties. That means that I gave my whole life to being in the Royal Canadian Mounted Police. Later on, I went in for healing the sick and all that sort of stuff. One way and another, I'm all tied up. I'm not available as an ordinary wife."

"Can't you even keep company then, miss?"

Mrs. Thoms scolded her son from her seat on the other side of the room, where she sat wringing a blood-stained towel in her hands.

"Do shut up, Nigel. You ain't never done, prying into other folk's business."

Francesca had picked up the needle holder and the child was apprehensive again.

"Are you going to put stitches in my leg now? Will it hurt me?"

"We call them sutures in the Mounties. They don't hurt a bit. You'll see."

She worked deftly and quickly. Esmond watched the concentration of her face and she looked up and caught him at it.

"Are you trying to see how the Mounties work, Dr. Ross?" she asked.

"Indeed, I think they work very well."

She put in the last stitch neatly and taped the dressing into position.

"Another cat scratch now and you'll not mind that, when you've been so brave about the rest of it. There! That's done."

She rinsed out the syringe, that had held the tetanus toxoid and dropped it back in the spirit, let out her breath in a long sigh.

"I think you'd better have a pocketful of those sweets from the tin, but don't go spreading the news of your award all over the school, or we'll never be done putting in sutures. . . ."

When Mrs. Thoms had taken her son off to his bed, Nurse Roberts looked round the big surgery.

"Will you divide the room into two, sir, to make an extra surgery? You'd only want a wall across the middle of it and a second door through to the waiting-room."

"The record cards would be difficult, Robbie. We'll have to get a receptionist. It came into my mind when I was watching you work together just now. You'd fit into the practice, when they retire you in six months. I assure you that you'd be most welcome to join . . . the Royal Canadian Mounted Police. . . ."

Connie came in to bring them the coffee and they all sat on in the surgery talking, making plans for a completely new lay out of the premises. There was a deep alcove in the waiting-room, which would make a perfect office for the receptionist and Nurse Roberts had accepted the post with alacrity. Connie suggested they get Tim Johnson, the brick-layer, to take on the task of alterations. He could do the work after hours with some of his mates and he was a tidy man, who would not make a mess with plaster all over the house. The conversation stretched on into the night hours and Francesca sat on the examination couch listening to it. After a while, she lay down for greater comfort, with their voices drifting away round her, busy with her own private thoughts.

Regent House was very different from her mirror image of it. She imagined the surgeries as they would be in a few weeks' time, divided into two, with cream walls and paintwork. There was a sombre atmosphere about the whole house, that cream paint would not lighten all the same. Esmond Ross was at the centre of it and the crux of the matter was that he did not know how to smile properly. His eyes were sad. Murdo had told her about him, the night she had confessed to him about her own dreadful affair. He had let slip that Esmond Ross of Harton was a similar case to her own . . . and then he had refused to tell her another word. They were two of a kind, she and this grave man, immune from love, by a different technique. If you loved somebody very much and lost them in death. . . . Perhaps he could be taught to smile again, rather after the manner of a crippled person, rehabilitated to walk again, using different sets of muscles.

There was a formidable task ahead of her, she thought, as she lay on the couch in a most unladylike way, with one knee crossed over the other, waggling her right ski boot in the air, to admire its blue eyelets. She must get the hang of general practice. It was vastly different to treating the sick in a hospital, where you had the power of a great institution at your back . . . facilities for tests, picked brains available for consultation at a moment's notice, nurses, with skill, patience and devotion. She turned her mind back to the lay out of the surgeries and thought of the waiting-room, as it would be, no longer

L-shaped, but with the big alcove trans-
formed to Nurse Roberts's office, separated
with a glass wall and a counter . . . like a
cinema cash desk, with a blind of coloured
slats.

She must be careful not to tread on
Connie's toes. Connie had been there for
years and years . . . had known Mrs. Ross . . .
had brought Pat up. It would take time for
her to settle down in Regent House, for she
had developed a restlessness, which never let
her stay in one place. It was caused by this
"vaccination against love." She must never
allow herself to be hurt again . . . never. The
First Gentleman was different, but you must
never trust a young man, who was like any
animal, stalking its prey. You dined and
wined and danced . . . kissed a little perhaps.
Then you moved on, before your feelings got
intense. Then you never faced the pain again.
It was strange all the same, the way she had
felt tonight, as if she were coming home. She
had been happier than she had been for years
and then Connie had told her it had all been a
mistake. She had felt as if Murdo had slammed
the door in her face that awful day at Oxford,
yet she could not understand why. Esmond
Ross was attractive to her. Perhaps she felt a

slight infatuation for him, like she had for the music master at St. Catherine's. . . .

Five minutes later, Ross stood by the couch and looked down at his new lady assistant, fast asleep, with her lashes making dark crescents against the planes of her cheeks. Seen like that, she seemed no older than Patricia. Yet she had awakened feelings in his heart, that he had believed to be dust and ashes. For a moment, he was back in the Queen Charlotte's Ball, a medical student . . . and Sheelagh was wearing a gown of white lace. He remembered the smooth gold of her hair and felt the burning pain in his chest . . . felt so completely unreal that he wondered if he had a fever. His cough was like a knife in his chest and Connie had come to stand beside him.

"God help her! She's tired out after that long journey . . . and you've brought on that old cough of yours, going in to the station tonight. I knew how it would be. I'm going to get Nurse Roberts to take your temperature, before she goes home . . . and if you've any sense in your head, you'll spend a day in bed tomorrow, sir and let Dr. Cunningham see to the practice. . . ."

Francesca found herself at a quarter to nine the next morning, in complete charge of the practice, standing in the gloomy old surgery again. She had a confused idea of where everything was and Connie to advise her on any doubtful point and she was dressed in a jumper and skirt of Pat's . . . and a pair of Connie's shoes, a size too big for her. It was an uncomfortable introduction to general practice. Still, she told herself that patients were patients, inside hospital or out, from Land's End to John o' Groats.

As the grandfather clock in the hall struck nine, she opened the door of the waiting-room and got the impression that there was no vacant seat. A ripple of surprise went over the room, as she appeared in the doorway.

"Good morning! I'm doing Dr. Ross's work today. I'm Francesca Cunningham. May I have the first patient, please?"

A woman near the entrance door got to her feet, staggering under the burden of a big child, wrapped in a blanket in her arms.

"They don't mind if I come in first, Nurse. It's an h'emergency. I really wanted the doctor himself. Ain't he better yet? I thought I saw him in the car last night."

91

The anxiety in her voice was reflected in every face in the waiting-room.

"Dr. Ross will be up and about in a day or two. I'm a doctor too. I expect I'll manage to help you."

The woman followed her into the surgery and gasped out the awful news.

"Our Cedric's swallowed a sixpence. Oh, God, miss, will he die?"

Francesca smiled at the worried face.

"If that's all that's wrong, I should put him down. He's far too big to carry. He must be six or seven and he's well up to digesting sixpence, but you'll get no interest on your money."

The woman's face was still anxious.

"You mean he won't die? He'll be all right? Do you really think he'll be all right?"

"I don't think it. I know it . . . and now, for heaven's sake, put him down before you strain your back."

The woman put Cedric down on the floor with a long-drawn sigh of relief. He was dressed in pink and white candy-striped pyjamas and his mother draped the blanket around his shoulders, Indian-fashion. He was completely unconcerned by her fears, as he wandered over to the desk, to remove the contents of the pigeon holes systematically.

"Drat it, Cedric! Will you leave them things alone?"

She might have been addressing the wall for all the notice her son took of her command, so she went over and dragged him roughly away by one arm.

"I'll give you a crack round the lug-hole, if you don't leave off . . . a big boy like you, frightening me half to death, with your dad on nights too."

She looked more harassed than ever as she glanced over at the doctor.

"His dad's on nights this week . . . twelve to ten . . . this would 'ave to 'appen. It were his dratted tooth . . . Cedric's tooth, I mean. He 'ad a loose one and the fairies was to leave sixpence. Found it as soon as he woke up. Trust 'im! He were sucking it, the little davil and it slip' down his froat. Will it go through 'im, or did you ought to pump 'im for it?"

"It'll go through with the greatest of ease," Francesca assured her and the child, who had moved to inspect the steriliser, chose that moment to commit a loud social error.

"Say 'pardon,' when you do that," the woman said, and went on automatically with the conversation.

"He's very small, you know. Are you quite sure it won't get jammed and 'ave to be cut out of him?"

"Quite sure . . . unless he changes it into six pennorth of coppers and then there might be some delay."

"Will I give him castor oil, Nurse . . . sorry, I mean Doctor . . . I forgot. Cedric, will you leave off playing with that machine. Else I'll come over there and do you! I never saw the like of the child. I reckon his father might be a chimpaneze monkey, with the tricks he gets up to. Leave off now, Cedric, do!"

The boy moved his attention to the dressing trolley.

"Saw them things on telly," he remarked and made another vulgar noise.

"I shouldn't give him castor oil," Francesca advised gravely. "You might be asking for trouble. Just have patience and if the fairies are good fairies, you'll get your moncy back tomorrow."

"Say 'pardon' when you do that," the woman scolded. "Where are your manners. Really, I'm that aerated at you this morning . . . and the washing not done yet, nor nothing."

94

"You'd better get along home then, and don't worry. He'll be fine. I promise you." Francesca said, holding the door open.

"And he's to have no medicine, Nurse, I mean, Doctor? There I go again, silly me!"

"Take him home and get him dressed. He can go to school as usual."

"I ain't taking him home, not till he's said 'pardon' . . . not if I'm to stay here all day. I don't know what his dad will 'ave to say to 'im, I'm sure . . . and before a lady doctor and all. . . ."

Francesca wondered what Dr. Ross might have said in the circumstances and unconsciously, she imitated his pedantic way of speaking.

"I think it might be as well to ignore such adventitious sounds, ma'am. I believe that is the accepted custom in the British Isles."

She accompanied her patient to the waiting-room door and was astonished to see it empty, except for one fat lady, who sat near the door.

"Where's everybody gone?"

"They don't hold with women doctors," the woman told her smugly. "They'll wait till the doctor himself is better. There's nothing wrong with them any road . . . and I don't mind seeing you for myself. I only want my ears syringing . . . Piggott's the name . . . Mrs. Ron Piggott."

She was between forty and fifty years of age and her hair was bleached to lifeless straw. Long purple ear-rings dangled two inches below the lobes of her ears, as she waddled into the surgery on high-heeled shoes, that looked two sizes too small under her fat calves.

"I'm not down for my weight today, but do you mind if I get on the scales all the same?"

She put down her bag, kicked off her shoes, climbed on the scales.

"My gawd! Seventeen stun still. Lucky the doctor himself isn't here . . . give me a bit of tongue pie. Still, I only want my ears syringing, so that's all right."

She sat down on the chair with a sigh of relief and her eyes twinkled like a pig's in her fat jolly face, through the purple and diamanté frames of her glasses.

"It's not what I eat makes me fat. It's being so content. That's what Mr. Piggott says. We don't hold with doctor's diets. . . ."

It took Francesca five minutes to find the record card, the auroscope, the kidney basin and the towel, and the woman's chatter was a background to her search.

"Fancy Dr. Ross taking up with a woman doctor! I suppose there isn't anything else you can get with the National Elf, only women and blackies, but I don't know what some of the Fen tigers will say when you walk into their bedrooms. Straight, I don't! Not but what some of the women will be glad to have another woman to talk to. What a man knows about having a baby, I can't never understand . . . and I expect you know about that, even if you haven't got a wedding ring on your finger. I 'unt have thought Dr. Ross would have had a woman in the house . . . not with his wife dead and that . . . must be dead this fifteen years, Sheelagh Ross . . . died when Pat was born. Her eyes were blue and her eyelashes as black as soot. Reckon she dyed them, because she was fair . . . gold-like. Still, handsome is as handsome does! She was smart with it too . . . best-dressed woman in the county, but it 'unt do her much good now . . . died in child-bed she did, poor thing!"

Connie's face peeped out through the kitchen door, as Francesca showed Mrs. Piggott out through the empty waiting-room.

"Your luggage came on the railway van and I kept the man here. I thought that you'd like to change into some of your own things. I can see you're not too happy as you are, and those shoes are falling off your feet. If you pick out what you want, they can take the rest of the luggage round to Nurse Robert's."

"There aren't many patients in the surgery this morning, Connie. At least there were, till I scared them away. It seems they don't approve of me."

She slipped out of the borrowed clothes and put on a white tweed suit and a dark green sweater. As she pushed her feet into green suede brogues, she felt that she had put on self-confidence too and Connie's voice boosted her morale.

"There hasn't been a lady doctor in the village as long as I can remember. They'll come round to the idea. You'll see. They'll welcome you with open arms, when they know you better . . . and the women and children will like coming to a lady. . . ."

She was disconcerted that her surgery consisted of only two patients, all the same, and the rounds did little to assure her. At house after house, she faced the look of surprise in the doorway, the grudging admission to the bedroom, the old men, who pulled the blankets up to their chins and regarded her with horror.

"Cor bugger! This is a rum do. Ain't the doctor well then?"

She had a call to make to a farm in Cotton Village, three miles away to see a Mrs. Parsons, who was suffering from arthritis. Old Farmer Parsons appraised her with bright eyes, that twinkled like periwinkles under jutting white brows and a shock of shaggy hair.

"Connie told me Dr. Esmond had got himself a gel, to help him in the practice, but it's hard to believe you're a qualified doctor . . . a young lass like you, no older than my grand-daughter."

She smiled at him ruefully and he saw the dimples round her mouth and sighed for his lost youth.

"I apologise for not being a little older, but time will take care of that for us. Dr. Ross will be better soon and he'll come and see you himself . . . though I don't know what help I'll be to him, if none of you will make do with me."

Her mouth drooped a little, but then she laughed at her predicament and old Parsons thought that her laughter brought the sun out in the sky and made the birds sing in the hedges.

"I assure you I passed my exams and I try very hard. Maybe I'll get by just this once, if you'll introduce me to the patient."

"Get by this once!" he echoed. "I like that! Reckon my old woman is tickled pink to have a woman to talk to. Women understand things better than men and they're a damn sight more conscientious and hard-working. Give me a bitch any day for a gun dog . . . won't have no other."

He conducted her up the stairs.

"Dr. Esmond's lucky to have a gel like you come to run the practice for him. Shouldn't surprise me a bit if he fell in love with them dimples o' yours and asked you to wed him. You're a change from Sheelagh Ross at any rate. Do you ride to hounds?"

She shook her head as they reached the landing and told him she had done a bit of hacking and been out cubbing a few times.

"I never see a woman the equal of Sheelagh Ross on the back of a horse . . . pretty as a picture too in a black habit . . . not built like a lad, same as you. I can see her now with her fair hair under her silk top hat and the stock white at her throat. Do anything with a horse, young Mrs. Ross could."

Old Mrs. Parsons was sitting up in bed, smiling a welcome to her.

"Don't listen to his chatter, Dr. Cunningham. Sheelagh took the laughter out of the doctor's eyes and I can tell you here and now, that you'll never take the laughter out of any man's eyes. Perhaps you'll put it back in his one of these days, but in the meantime, I have a tall order for you today . . . a pair of new knees and a set of new shoulders and wrists. I'm lying up here like an old log and there's all the work of a farm kitchen waiting for me below-stairs."

Francesca came up against one of the strangest of the "Fen tigers" that evening and she did not score any great success with him. It was just like medicine, she thought, that such a situation should blow up on her first day in the practice. She started surgery at six o'clock and took in Nigel Thoms from a full waiting-room. Nigel had come to get his dressings changed and he arrived into the consulting room, hopping along on one leg, with his face split into a melon-seed grin, and his mother walking at his heels.

"Never had such an easy job getting our Nigel to the doctor's before," the woman declared. "If that had been Dr. Ross, he'd have started his blaring at our front gate. You've got a way with you, miss, and that's a fact, but you're not like a real doctor at all. I expect that's what it is."

"That's a strange back-handed compliment, Mrs. Thoms, if it's intended for a compliment in the first place."

The woman settled herself comfortably into the chair.

"That it is, miss. Why, a person wouldn't think they was going to the doctor, coming down here to talk to you. That little old boy had me 'aerated' the whole day, asking was it time to go down to surgery . . . seems 'e wants to hear some more about them Mounties. . . ."

She expected at least one or two of the patients to wait to see her, but the room was empty when she took Nigel out. She walked back slowly to sit at her desk with her head in her hands. There was just no demand for a female doctor. It was obvious what would happen if they had two surgeries, running together. Dr. Ross's would be full and hers empty. She felt angry at the prejudice, that still existed in a country area against women in medicine. Even the worst of the male doctors would have been preferred to the most brilliant of the ladies . . . not that she was brilliant or anything like it. There was a knock at the door and Connie came in, her face more serious than Francesca had seen it.

"Zachary Monk and his wife came to the back door just now, Doctor. They wouldn't go round to the waiting-room in case people talked. It's the luck of the devil that this had to happen with himself up in bed. Monk was against seeing you, but I said I'd tell you and you'd know what to do. A terrible thing has happened. . . ."

Francesca sat at the desk and listened to the story and thought that at least, with an empty waiting-room outside, she had plenty of time to deal with the situation.

"They brought Rachael down. She's their one ewe lamb and she's barely sixteen. She was having a wash after tea and her mother walked in on her and thought her stomach was big. They've been arguing back and forth for hours . . . and now, Rachael has admitted she's expecting a baby . . ."

"Is that all it is, Mistress Constance? Ewe lambs have been known to be pregnant before now. It's a fairly common occurrence and I'll deal with it comfortably. . . ."

"There's more to it than that . . ." Connie sighed and shook her head. "There was a police case a few weeks back, but we all thought it over and done with. Rachael swore that everything was regular and we hoped she'd forget her experience in time, poor thing . . . one of the nicest, quietest girls in Harton, and it had to be her it happened to. A madman he was and she met him coming home from work one night . . . lonely road and not a soul to go to her aid, God have pity on her! They locked him up in the asylum after and that's where he'll be for the rest of his life, but the Monks are a queer lot. They don't cook on Sundays, nor go to the pictures or dances. They don't smoke or drink. Rachael was no older than Pat is now, when it happened . . . barely out of school and in a job behind the counter in Marks. . . ."

"I'd better get this straight, Connie. Rachael Monk was criminally assaulted a few months ago and a man was convicted of the offence and is serving a sentence in a criminal lunatic asylum. Is that it?"

"She was in a terrible state that night, when they brought her in . . . all cuts and bruises. Dr. Esmond sent her straight off to hospital. She was half out of her mind with the fright of it . . . and now she says she's pregnant. I don't know whether she's right about that or not."

"We'd best have her in here and find out then."

Connie looked at her doubtfully.

"I don't know what Monk will say to that. He doesn't approve of women."

Francesca stood up from the desk and pushed her hands deep in the pockets of her white coat. Her face was grim.

"I've met so many people in the last twenty-four hours that don't approve of women, that even I am beginning not to find it a joke any more. You'd best show them in and tell the vast crowd in the waiting-room that I'll be delayed a bit. Master Monk will have more on his mind tonight, than to bother about the sex of the medical attendant."

Rachael Monk was indeed only a child, Francesca thought, as she saw the small woe-begone face, the snub pixie nose, the hair that gleamed very gold in the light. Monk walked in very grimly, with his wife at his heels, a sturdy country woman, with greyish hair, eyes red with weeping. Monk stopped up short and looked blackly at Francesca.

"Doctoring is queer work for a woman . . . ain't never seen a lady doctor before."

"Don't you think that a woman might be the person of choice to deal with a case, caused by the wickedness of man?" she shot out at him and then forced herself not to feel angry about his prejudice. "Besides, I had a young lad in here just now, who thinks I'm not like a proper doctor at all. Perhaps Rachael will share his opinion and be willing to talk to me? I'll help her all I can."

She glanced down at the panel record that Connie had found for her in the files.

"You think Rachael is expecting a baby? Is that it?"

He stood with his legs straddled apart and stared at her stonily.

"My gel is a sinner like us all. Jehovah is stretching out His hand to chastise her. We are all born in sin and He stretched out his hand to punish the evil doers. If He has thought to lay a burden upon our shoulders, we must bear it and praise His Name. . . ."

"You'd better wait outside in the kitchen with Connie and let your wife stay here while I examine Rachael. It's women's work after all, and if the Lord has seen fit to punish the poor child for something she never did, it's time we knew about it."

He glared at her, as he turned to go with Connie.

"That's sacriligious talk. You ought to pray forgiveness on your bended knees. . . ."

Connie was sheep-dogging him out of the room, but he went unwillingly, looking back at her over his shoulder and muttering under his breath. Francesca put him out of her mind and set about talking to Rachael, but the girl was terrified and wept into her sodden handkerchief.

"Don't you know the only wrong you're guilty of is keeping all this to yourself?" Francesca asked her at last and the tear-drenched eyes lifted to hers.

"I didn't want them to know. It'll kill Dad. I'd rather be in my grave than bring sorrow to him and Mum. I wanted to kill myself, but I wasn't brave. . . ."

"That wouldn't do any good to anybody and well you know it. You were brave enough to try to take all the trouble on your own shoulders and try to save them pain, but you can't tackle this sort of thing by yourself.

We're all here to help you . . . and to share the sorrow with you."

The girl turned her head and her tears dripped slowly down on the pillow slip to make grey circles against the linen.

"There ain't nobody to help me only Jehovah. I wish He'd take me away out of it all. Then I'd not have to face the shame, with everybody pointing a finger at me saying "Rachael Monk is going to have a baby. . . .""

The examination was finished at last and Francesca went to sit at her desk and looked across at Mrs. Monk.

"It's no false alarm, but it's nothing we can't face together."

The woman put her head in her hands and wept silently and Francesca turned to the girl, who had come to stand by her mother.

"You're not in disgrace, Rachael. Put that idea out of your head. Without you, your mother and father would have nothing left in the world. . . ."

She spoke for a long time, but she could get no response, except the words repeated over and over again.

"I'll kill myself and put an end to it. That's what I'll do . . . kill myself and put an end to it. . . ."

She sent them out to the kitchen eventually, cursing her luck in being presented with such a case. She had no knowledge of Dr. Ross's views about the ethics of the situation and he was in no fit state to be worried with it. She must stand upon her own feet and do as she thought fit. When Monk came back to the surgery, he scowled at her in a way that boded ill for the interview, and she thought that he looked a little like the God of the Old Testament himself, with his granite face and jutting brows. She felt as unsure of herself professionally as she had ever felt, as she leaned her elbows on the desk and told him the findings of the case.

"There are several things to be considered, Mr. Monk. There was a case like this in London some years ago, where a young girl was assaulted by soldiers. It was decided that she would be damaged mentally, if her pregnancy was allowed to continue. . . ."

His voice was harsh as he broke in on her roughly.

"You're saying that you'd be prepared to take the baby away. That ain't a right thing for a doctor to say."

There was pain in his eyes and anger too.

Sorrow had pulled down all the lines of his face in despair.

"It might be the best thing to do. It might not," she told him wearily. "It's tremendously complicated, both medically and legally. It would only be decided at specialist level. . . ."

She was tired and dispirited herself. She knew she was not talking to this simple man in terms he could understand and she wished she could get up and walk out of the room and leave the whole case to be somebody else's responsibility.

"There's Rachael to be thought of . . . and you and your wife . . . and lastly there's the child itself. . . ."

"There you have it, miss," the man said grimly. "You should ha' put the child first . . . not last. It's the important one, ain't it?"

"I'd like to send Rachael in to see a specialist in mental diseases. . . ." she began, but again, he burst in upon her rudely and angrily.

"You're saying my gel is mad? Is that it?"

She shook her head and made no reply and he went on, "They murder babies at the hospital now, do they?"

She knew she was making a mess of the whole affair, as he stood up abruptly, twisting his cap round in his hands, scowling down at her with menace in his face.

"I think you should know there's a good chance of your daughter taking her own life from despair. What then?"

He strode to the door and then turned back, his voice strident and over bearing.

"She'd go to hell. That's what. It's a sin to take what belongs to the Almighty. I brung my gel up to know that. She knows she'd have destroyed another soul and that she'd burn in hell fires for all eternity . . . along of her bastard. She's talking daft, do she talk like that. I'll take off my belt and let her feel the buckle end of it across her back."

"The father of this coming infant is mentally ill," she reminded him, in a voice that sounded quiet after his ranting. "It's hereditary illness. This baby might be better never to have lived. . . ."

He came across to the desk and banged his hand down almost under her nose.

"Who are you to be the judge of that? Are you setting yourself up above Jehovah to say who's to live and who's to die? You're a sinful young woman. Does Dr. Ross know he's taken up with a woman, that holds the views, you've been airing here tonight?"

She met his eyes squarely.

"Dr. Ross would agree with me . . . most doctors would. I told you the decision would not be made by us. You'd have to see the specialists. They'd say what was to be done for the best. . . ."

"Tha's the easy way out of it. Satan is a-whispering in my ear to let you do it. I'd expect a flibberty gibbet of a gel like you are, to suggest that sort of thing, but it 'ont wash. Suppose the child is a lunatic? Suppose it spends all its normal life in a lunatic asylum? Ain't it got all eternity with the Good Shepherd? This life is over in the twinkling of an eye, but eternity goes on for ever."

"That's on one side of the scales. In the other is unhappiness for your whole family. Go home and think it over. We'll talk about it tomorrow and the next day . . . the day after that. I don't want to fight with you. I want to help you. . . ."

She saw them off at last, letting them out through the front door. Then she went back into the surgery and washed her hands at the basin, wondering if after all, she was like Pontius Pilate. Who was to say that Monk's

112

views were not the correct ones? She felt shaken by the stormy interview and was glad that there were no more problems for her to solve. Then Connie came round the door and she was smiling again.

"It seems that you dealt with Zachary Monk then, Dr. Frankie? Isn't it time you were starting at your surgery again? The waiting-room is packed to the doors with ladies. It seems to have got out that we have a lady assistant. Everyone for miles around with a female complaint is outside, waiting for your advice. I'd say you've got two hours work ahead of you . . . and me with a cheese *soufflé* in the oven for dinner. If it's not eaten the minute it's dished, it will fall flat on its face."

"Never mind, Mistress Constance, I'll buy you a new one."

Connie's eyes went up to the ceiling, as she declared it might be Dr. Murdo himself speaking.

"It's all very well to laugh, but what will Dr. Ross say to me? He's getting out of his bed this minute, after Dr. Jones telling him not to get up for two days . . . just to have dinner with you. There's a compliment for you, madam. I never saw him so taken with anybody, as he is with yourself. On top of that, Tim Johnson, the bricklayer, was down to the back door just now. He's to start on the surgeries tomorrow, so we'll all be up to our necks in bricks and mortar for the next two months . . . and all you can do is to stand there and make jokes about it all."

Two hours later, she smiled at Esmond Ross down the length of the dining-table, thinking how rich a colour the red of his velvet smoking jacket was, as it reflected in the old mahogany.

"Indeed, you'll not go back to work tomorrow, sir. Connie won't permit it and you told me five minutes ago that you're afraid of her."

"But you can't manage——"

"Oh, yes I can. I may turn the practice into one huge gynaecological unit, and I may frighten some Fen tigers out of their wits, and I assure you that both these possibilities are highly likely."

She stretched her arms above her head and laughed, and again, he thought what a pleasant sound it was, for it seemed to sparkle through the gloom of the old house and bring gaiety into every corner.

"It's not that I'm afraid you can't cope with

the practice. You did splendidly today and I'm quite confident that your work is excellent in every way."

She laughed again and then pretended to be rueful. She was trying to get him to smile and well he knew it.

" 'Cope' isn't the word. I got by, today, but I didn't 'cope.' Oh, Lord, Dr. Ross, it would have been far better, if you had taken up shooting and wanted a gun dog . . . and if I was a Labrador Retriever like the one at the Post Office Stores. Do you know what old Farmer Parsons said to me today? I've been saving it up to tell you . . . his opinion on gun dogs. It doesn't apply to the medical profession, more's the pity. I only wish it did. . . ."

Within six weeks, the surgery alterations were finished, and a very uncomfortable time it had been, with piles of bricks and heaps of rubble in the background of most of the consultations. Two days after Tim Johnson's labour forces had withdrawn, Francesca drove up in her M.G. and let herself into the house to take her surgery. She felt very much at home by this time and she took off her suede jacket and threw it on the hall seat, before she poked her head into the dining-room, where Esmond was finishing his break-fast. He stood up to greet her and she moved over to stand with her back to the fire.

"It's better weather today, Dr. Ross. Looks as if it's going to be fine for Pat's half-term."

He glanced down at his *Times* and told her rather absent-mindedly that Patricia never came home for half-term.

"It's not worth it."

"Not worth it!" she echoed in scorn. "All the girls go home, except the poor little miseries with overseas parents. I always went home to Murdo. It was better than the real holidays in a way. It was all so concentrated. We did something special every single day."

"Such as?" he asked with one eyebrow raised in her direction and she grinned at him like a schoolboy.

"Once we went straight off to London. We saw six theatre shows. It's possible if you go to matinées. We saw a picture or two in addition, because we were making a record. The girls at St. Catherine's were green with envy. It was worth it, even if Murdo and I were a bit exhausted. You have no idea of the importance of half-term. Besides, I haven't met Pat yet, you know, although we do cor-

116

respond. Oh, Dr. Ross, please let her come home."

"You think she'd like to?"

"I had a letter from Murdo the day after he took her back. I didn't tell you . . . didn't want to make you sad too. Murdo said that she 'greeted a wee bit,' as they left Harton and he had to pretend not to notice it."

"We shall certainly have her home then. It was not apparent to me that you girls set so much importance on your fathers."

He paused abruptly.

"I beg your pardon, Francesca. I wouldn't have said that . . . May I substitute the word 'homes'?"

"It wasn't home that was important. It was Murdo for me and it's Pat for you. Don't feel put out about mentioning fathers. The First Gentleman was fine . . . still is. I never felt the least bit deprived. He had a discreet word with me about self-pity early on and he never treated me as a child . . . at least hardly ever."

She looked rather awkward for a moment and confessed that she had made all the arrangements to have Pat home and said she was glad he agreed.

"I knew you wouldn't refuse. Will you

drive me over, when you go to fetch her? I'd like to see St. Catherine's again."

"Really, Francesca! I can't take time off to go over there. In any case, we can't both leave the practice. It would have been enjoyable to go all the same."

He admitted to himself as he spoke, that he would have enjoyed the long drive alone with her. He found her a pleasant amusing companion. She had put her hands in the pockets of her green dress and was looking down at the toes of her shoes.

"Actually that's all fixed up too. Alex Brough is off duty in the General and he'll cover for us. I enlisted Connie's help. She's longing to have Pat home too. Alex is going to bring his Staff Nurse here to dinner. We won't be home till very late, for I know you'll want to go on to Oxford and look in on Murdo. . . ."

"You seem to have been very busy," he remarked dryly. "What if I change my mind and say we can't go?"

She only laughed at him and went off towards the door. Then she turned back to talk to him again.

"There's another important matter I wanted to discuss. I know one should never carry tales, but this is for the good of the entire Harton School. I'd better tell you now and call a halt to a nefarious practice. For it's time you stopped paying ransom on the person of your beloved Simon."

"What on earth are you talking about now?"

She walked slowly back to the fire.

"One day last week, Simon was lost and a child brought him back . . . and was rewarded, perhaps justly, perhaps not, with the noble sum of a shilling. Then a day or two later, he disappeared again, and this time, he was brought back by three children, who were fortunate enough to meet you . . . and received a shilling each."

"They were very kind to go to the trouble of bringing him home. I don't know why he's started to stray."

"But I do! Yesterday, he did it again and he was returned by a host of children. I was there myself. I saw them. There was a small gentleman behind all the others, who carried the tail . . . like a train."

His eyes were beginning to smile at last, when she put on these acts for his amusement. She shook her head reprovingly.

"You hadn't any change. You gave them a

119

ten shilling note and you stipulated particularly that the small gentleman with the tail should not be short-changed, because of his tender age."

"Indeed I did," he laughed.

"One mustn't stand by and see dishonesty rewarded. I can't divulge the source of my information, but I found out that poor Simmy is the victim of abduction. I discovered something quite horrible."

"Which was?" he asked her gravely.

"A very ancient kipper on a long string is thrown over your boundary wall. They haven't ploughed back the profits into the business, so I'm afraid it is the original kipper. I'm horrified that the dignified Simon could feel himself attracted to such an object, but he does. They catch him with it, like a salmon. They lie in wait for him. They were most surprised last evening, when they caught me instead. I don't think it will occur again, but it might. I buried the kipper for one thing and they may not have the capital to set up in trade again. If they try it on though, perhaps you could hand out a limited number of medium slaps across their rear ends . . . instead of largesse. That would have been the judgement of Murdo."

She thought quite suddenly that he was smiling at her, as if he liked her.

"I'll see to it personally," he assured her. "But I don't think we should tell Connie. When you think of the care she takes of his . . . liver."

Francesca had picked the cat up in her arms and was talking to him, apologising to him for telling tales.

"There are standards of decency, Simon . . . and besides Murdo won't find out I told."

"What's he got to do with it?" Esmond asked her as they walked out together towards the surgeries.

"I'll tell you one of these days. It was a painful experience . . . and incidentally, if you are called upon to execute judgement on the felons, I think that Murdo would have granted an amnesty to the small gentleman with the tail. The sight of execution would deter him sufficiently. At least, that's what Murdo would have said."

Simon had jumped up on his desk to sit beside the blotter in his customary position and Nurse Roberts came bustling starchily into the room. She had got permission from the Nursing Association to start her retirement early . . . or rather her part-time retirement, for she still attended the midwifery cases.

"There's an accident case for you, Dr. Ross, but it's not urgent. Will you ring when you're ready to start?"

Francesca had turned back to speak to him again.

"By the way, I've asked Mrs. Graves to bring Teddy up this morning. I'm not very happy about him. I'd be awfully glad of your help. . . ."

She took herself off and he sat at his desk, knowing that he would hurry through his patients, so that he could go into her surgery early. He enjoyed seeing her tackle the problems of general practice and she had a way of sharing the funny side of things with him. She would look across at him as if to say "Life is not all sadness. Look here . . . and here." There was no doubt that she had an aura of happiness, that moved about her like a cloud. He had noticed himself hurrying home to lunch just to be with her. He enjoyed her wrangling with Connie too. There was a perpetual battle of wits between them, for Connie was heavily infected by her gaiety. He had been very foolish to resent the coming of a woman doctor. She had proved herself as

122

good, if not better, than any man would have been and she was a very able clinician. He rang the bell for his first patient and Nurse Roberts brought in a boy, holding a blood-stained handkerchief to his mouth. Behind came the mother, a grim expression on her face.

"Accident prone, you said he was, Dr. Ross, and you were quite right. Just look at him now. His dad will murder him, when I take him home."

Esmond glanced at the panel record that the nurse laid at his hand and saw that his old friend, James Knights, had reached the age of ten. He was the butcher's son and Knights always declared that Jimmy was as good a customer of the doctor's, as the doctor was of his, for he never seemed to be without a cut or a bruise on some part of his small wiry body.

"Rode his bike into a parked car," grumbled Mrs. Knights. "He's knocked his front teeth out this time. He hadn't got his mind on what he was doing. It's the same old story."

She looked aggrievedly at her son as the nurse helped him climb up on the examination couch.

"One of these days, you'll ride under a bus on that bike of yours and get yourself killed. Then don't say I didn't warn you. You just can't keep your mind on what you're doing. I never saw such a young Turk."

The two central top teeth had vanished and the laterals were broken down to jagged edges.

"You've really been in the wars this time, young man," Esmond said. "I'm afraid I'll have to send you in to the Dental Out-patients, but they're old friends of yours, so you won't mind that. We'll have to have an X-ray of your mouth too, but you're well known in X-ray. Your lip came off very lightly, considering what you've done to those teeth."

He smiled at the boy.

"Nurse will give you a tetanus booster before you go, but I needn't tell you about that either. You know the drill."

He went back to the desk to write the letter and Jimmy looked across at his mother.

"I had my mind on what I was doing," he mumbled defensively and Mrs. Knights looked indignant.

"You couldn't have and that's a fact. That car wasn't even moving. It was parked by the

124

side of the road and you went straight slap bang into it."

"I had my mind on reading my comic. That's why I rode into the car. I never saw it. . . ."

It would have been one of Francesca's funny situations in life, Esmond thought, and he would tell her about it over lunch, to see her smile. He would not have thought it funny two months ago, just stupid and rather boring.

"Reading a comic and riding your bike at the same time!" Mrs. Knights was complaining in the background. "Reckon you'd better keep that from your dad."

His next patient was Ron Piggott. Nurse Roberts put his record card on the desk and withdrew quietly.

"Good morning, Piggott. It's a better day today."

The man's double chin quivered and he looked at the doctor out of miserable eyes.

"I suppose it is for some. It couldn't be wusser for me. I'm in nice trouble at home, I can tell you. I didn't know what to do about it. Straight I didn't."

He sank his sixteen stone of flabby body into the chair with a sigh.

"Then I thought I'd take it down to you, sir. I said to myself, 'Young Dr. Ross will put me right, if anybody can'."

He was one of the patients, who still thought of Esmond as the young doctor, having known his father all their lives. He took out a pocket book, which bulged as much as he did himself, and extracted a cheap white envelope. Holding it gingerly between finger and thumb, he brought it across the room and laid it at Esmond's hand.

"That come on the morning post. It were addressed to the missus . . . and she opened it, worse luck!"

He mopped his sweating brow with a red-spotted handkerchief and went back to sink on to his chair, his legs straddled apart and his bow window of a stomach comfortably filling any semblance of a lap he might possess.

"Cor love you, Doctor! It fair turned my stomach to read what's wrote in there . . . and my missus carried on. I never saw her take on like it before. . . ."

Esmond had taken the letter from its envelope and had put on his heavy horn-rimmed glasses to read it. It consisted of a sheet of the cheapest ruled note-paper and

126

somebody had gummed words on it, that looked as if they had been cut from a book or a newspaper. In some places, perhaps where a word had been impossible to find, it was filled in with writing of a childish type . . . block letters all tumbled together higgledy-piggledy.

"Dear Mrs. Piggott,
I am writing as a friend to warn you that your husband is carrying on with another woman. He is as fat as a fool, but that doesn't stop him behaving like a tom cat . . . and to be carnally minded is death. . . ."

Esmond read on from one filthy accusation to the next till he finally came to the signature "a friend." He took off his glasses and laid them on the desk, before he looked across the room at his patient.

"I take it there is no truth in any part of this? I am bound to put that question to you."

The man's face flushed a dull painful red.

"Cor bugger, Dr. Esmond! I never done the like of that. You're not thinking me capable of——"

"Of course not. I've known you all my life.

Besides, that you and your good lady are far too happy for anything in the revolting document to be true."

He pushed it away from him with an index finger, his mouth grimacing in disgust.

"I suppose we should hand it over to the police without delay. These anonymous letters very rarely come singly. We may have quite an epidemic of the wretched things and the police will put a stop to them. I'll drop in and have a word with your wife first and get her views about the whole matter. I promise you I'll put her mind at rest and for the moment, I'll keep this letter, if I may."

"I don't never want to see it again, bloomin' thing. She'll be glad to see you, I can tell you . . . been blaring ever since it come this morning. She'd not even eat her breakfast. . . ."

At least that might do some good, Esmond thought dryly, remembering the lady, who was even fatter than her husband and who could never be induced to stay on her reducing diet.

"She 'unt let it go to the police though. She 'unt want Sergeant Bullen to see the like o' that."

"I'm not sure that I shouldn't burn it,"

Esmond said as he locked the letter into a drawer. "Still it will be safe in here for the moment. Now go home and tell your wife I'm ashamed of her, not to have more faith in you. I'll give her a talking to, when I see her. . . ."

The man stood up in a shame-faced way and went towards the door.

"I knew you'd sort it out, sir. You always put us right. I dunno what we'd do in Harton without you to get us out of our troubles. Your old dad was just the same. . . ."

Ellen Ferguson, the housekeeper from the Grange was the next patient and she had come about her employer, Miss Mallory, an eccentric old martinet of seventy odd years. Ellen must be seventy herself, Esmond thought, as he greeted her.

"Miss Mallory told me to knock at the front door," she quavered apologetically. "She's a private patient, she says, and she must be seen to before the panel patients, but of course, I did no such thing."

Her prim mouth draw-stringed in, as she sat down, a thin, scrawny woman, with a purple-veined nose and a lantern jaw. Her pince-nez glasses ran out from a round button, pinned to her bosom and her false teeth were so big and ill-fitting, that they slipped up and down as she talked.

"I've just come to fetch her prescription, but I thought I'd ask you to drop in to see her one day on your rounds. You mustn't say that I asked you to do it, or she'd be put out with me, but I'm worried about her, doctor."

"And why is that, Ellen?"

"She's so restless at night. She wanders about the house, if I don't watch her. Back in her girlhood, she is sometimes, laughing and singing. I keep my door open, but I'm terrified I might miss her. She could fall down the stairs and kill herself."

"Have you told Mr. Lucien about it?"

"Of course, I've told him," she said, her mouth compressed with her disapproval of Miss Mallory's grand-nephew. "I'm afraid he's not much help, sir. It's never been a secret what Mr. Lucien is like. He doesn't care a pin for my poor lady. All he wants is to get his hands on her fortune, when she's gone . . . though I wouldn't say that to anybody else but yourself. . . ."

He ran through the rest of the patients quickly and rang for Nurse Roberts.

"Will you tell my colleague that I'm at her

disposal and ask if I may sit in on the rest of her surgery?"

That would make Dr. Cunningham nervous, the nurse thought. She might hide it almost completely, but she was self-conscious when he was in the room. She did not seem able to forget he was there and her eyes would keep darting to his face to see whether he approved an action or disapproved. Anyone with half an eye in his head could see he approved everything she did.

"I'm afraid Dr. Ross is finished before you, Dr. Frankie. He wants to come in."

The lady doctor made a little grimace and asked her what patients there were left to see.

"Miss Moss, Billy Binns. Teddy Graves isn't here yet, but he'll be along soon. Mrs. Graves is always on time."

She was sitting at the lovely old table desk, that she had brought from Oxford and Esmond stood for a moment, leaning on his walking stick, with Simon rubbing himself against his ankles.

"Would you like to come and sit by me?"

"Indeed, I would."

That was very true, he thought, as he crossed the room to sit at the far end of the desk. He admitted to himself that he had hurried through the patients, just to be with her. He caught the familiar cut-pencil sophistication of the scent she always used, as she smiled at him.

"It's Miss Moss first . . . not very interesting, I'm afraid, but you know her far better than I do."

Francesca wondered if Esmond had a fellow-feeling for Miss Moss, because she walked on a stick, not so gracefully as he did, but on a stick all the same, with an ugly up-and-down bobbing movement. She had a deaf aid, pinned to the front of her winter coat, where it crackled and whistled like a bad wireless set.

"Good morning, Miss Moss. It's nice to see you looking so well."

"Of course, it's all right if he stays in the surgery, Miss Cunningham. I saw him before ever you came and he's a very clever young man."

Francesca went over to speak close to the old lady's ear.

"Are you getting along any better with your deaf aid now?"

"Oh, nothing much!" Miss Moss smiled. "It's only the screws in my poor legs, as it always is."

This would happen when King Cophetua was in the room, thought Francesca, putting out a finger to tap the deaf aid.

"I-don't-think-this-is-switched-on," she said slowly and distinctly and the patient took it in her hand and twiddled a knob.

"That's my deaf aid. Haven't you seen one like that? I expect you're used to the National Health ones, but this is a good one. I've had it ten years. A lovely young gentleman came to the house to fit me out . . . said it was the latest model, but it goes on and off . . . especially in the sermon, when I want it. It's all right today though."

"Why can't you hear what I say then?"

"No, my ears are fine, but it's nice of you to ask."

Francesca looked ruefully at Esmond and shook her head, for he was obviously enjoying her predicament. She turned back to her patient and tried again, more loudly than before.

"What's the trouble today?"

"You mustn't mumble so. All the young people mumble these days and it's very bad manners."

"I suppose one must look on the bright side and remind oneself that it's not a busy day,"

133

Francesca murmured to Nurse Roberts, who was tidying a pile of enamel bowls away into the instrument cabinet. "Am I supposed to send out a smoke signal next?"

She took the battery of the deaf aid in her hand and shook it vigorously, muttering under her breath that it was time Miss Moss's lovely young man paid her another visit and fitted her out again.

"He won't come again," Miss Moss beamed. "He told me all I want to keep me going is a new battery."

The nurse had come across to look with interest at the proceedings, as the deaf aid began to whistle and crackle more loudly than ever.

"What did you do with it, Dr. Frankie? You made it work just then."

"I shook it, but she sounds as if she's broadcasting now. I wonder if it's the Third Programme."

"I can hear every word you ladies are saying," the old lady piped up. "And I'm not broadcasting either . . . first, second, or third programme and my battery's not run down . . . bought it in the Post Office Stores day before yesterday."

"Are your knees any better?" Francesca put in quickly.

"Of course they're no better. That stuff you gave me isn't a mite of good. It didn't make any difference to 'em, any more than what the doctor himself has been giving me for twenty years, nor his dad before him."

Dr. Ross thought it time to come to the rescue. He leaned a little forward and spoke clearly.

"What about some more physiotherapy?" he suggested and the old lady's hand went up to cup her ear.

"Some what, Dr. Esmond?"

"Some physiotherapy at the hospital."

"I'm not going into that hospital again and it's no use to send me. The nurses stole my shoes and I never got them again."

Francesca stood squarely in front of her with her hands thrust into the pockets of her white coat.

"You know that's not true. You told me last month that Dr. Ross stole your combinations and what do you think he wanted them for?"

Miss Moss looked at her stubbornly.

"Can't hear you now. Dratted thing's gone

135

off again, like it does in the middle of Vicar's sermon."

The whistling and the crackling died abruptly away as Francesca gave the deaf aid a prolonged shake once again.

"Hey! It's gone dead altogether now. You've used up the battery treating it like that. It didn't ought to be shook."

"Heaven send me patience!"

The girl was back at the desk, her dark hair falling over her brow, as she bent her head. She went back to hold a sheet of paper out.

"Do you want any more tablets or medicine? I've written it out for you to read."

"You might as well have saved yourself the trouble, dear. I haven't got my reading glasses by me."

"Tablets? Linament? Medicine?"

"That's what I came down for. Wish they did me some good."

Francesca was writing out the prescription at the desk and her voice reached Esmond's ear faintly.

"How do you spell 'strychnine,' sir . . . or 'arsenic'?"

She went back to pass the form to the old lady and shook her head.

"You're a wicked old woman! You only

136

hear what you want to hear, but I've given you your drugs. If the linament does nothing else, it will keep the moth out of the knees of your comms. If Dr. Ross stole one pair, you'd best be careful of the ones you have left."

The woman was chortling with glee, bent double, striking her hand against her thigh.

"That's a rich one, that is! You've got yourself a lovely young lady, Doctor, it's a tonic to come and see her. Keep the moth out of my comms indeed! That's good! Well, dear, may you laugh for many a year to come, for you're a right bonnie maid. Keep the moth out of my comms indeed! That's a nice thing for a doctor to say to a patient."

She hobbled out of the room and Esmond grumbled at his assistant.

"It would sound rich in front of the Disciplinary Committee, if she lodged a complaint."

She threw back her head and laughed.

"That I'd like to see . . . really and truly . . . Miss Moss giving evidence before the Committee. Then they'd see what the poor old G.P. has to cope with."

Nurse Roberts smiled at her happy face.

"Mrs. Binns is down with Billy's impetigo. She says it's no better, but she's not being getting the crusts off before she put the ointment on."

"Not the slightest bit better?" Francesca asked Mrs. Binns a moment later and the woman looked at her guardedly.

"I wouldn't say no better, but it ain't all that better."

When the consultation was over, the nurse held out the sweet jar to Billy and the boy took a handful and experienced "the paw in the bottle" problem and had to relinquish half his spoils. He tore the paper off one of the sweets and jammed it into his mouth, when he had put the rest in his pocket and then he discarded the paper carelessly on the floor.

"It's as well to use the waste paper basket," Esmond reminded him and Billy picked up the paper and did as he was told.

"We can't begin too early to teach them good habits," Nurse Roberts said, nodding her head in approval, and Mrs. Binns raised her eyes to the ceiling.

"That boy would want a hundred black slaves to wait on him. He leaves his things all over the house, mostly where his dad treads on them . . . on the stairs most likely, and then there's hell to pay."

138

Francesca walked across to open the door and then noticed that Esmond was looking at something with a very fixed stare. She turned back to see Billy picking his nose delicately. He removed whatever it was he sought and rolled it between finger and thumb with great concentration in what the physicians call the "pill-rolling movement." Then he walked over to the waste paper basket and deposited it therein, while Mrs. Binns watched him complacently.

"He's showing willing, as we say in the Fens," Francesca sighed. "If he keeps to that standard of tidiness, think what a great husband he'll make. . . ."

Her face was serious suddenly, as she closed the door behind Mrs. Binns's back.

"But our third case is a bird of a different hue. I'm afraid I've struck a spot of tragedy. I hope not, but . . ."

She leaned against the edge of the desk, her eyes sad.

"Nurse Roberts says Teddy Graves is here. You may remember sending him to hospital six months ago. They had a look at him and thought he might be just a bad walker. Nothing was found on X-ray and all his tests were normal."

"Indeed I remember. They thought that Mrs. Graves overstated the case and that Teddy was playing up to the fuss. They're to see him again in six months. That should be about now. He's a clumsy little chap and he stumbles easily, but he never complains."

"I had a look at him when they came for the letter for the hospital last night. I'm afraid something sinister has developed. His sense of balance is bad and he can't run. I tried him out in the drive. Then I put him on the couch and made him lie flat, asked him to sit up. He couldn't do it. He could hardly turn himself over. His leg and arm muscles have got weaker over the past six months. . . ."

He raised his eyebrows at her.

"So!"

"So he's got pseudo-hypertrophic muscular atrophy, sir. I'm almost sure of it. I hope I'm wrong. You may disagree. . . ."

Teddy Graves rolled into the room like a sailor, grinning all over his fat jolly face, as he saw Simon on the desk.

"Goo you on now, Simmy. How many rats you caught today? Not as many as our old Whiskers! He caught a big rat, Dr. Frankie . . . last week he caught it . . . brought it into the kitchen to show it to Mum. She didn't half let fly. Does Simmy catch rats?"

"Simon catches kippers, Teddy."

"Goo you on, miss. You're pulling my leg. . . ."

"Now then, Teddy, up on the couch with you! Dr. Ross wants to have a look at you. Then we'll pick out some of your favourite mint toffees."

The boy was very overweight, thought Ross. His legs and arms looked powerful, but they were the reverse.

"He never walked till he was eighteen months, sir. You remember. I nearly lost him, when I was carrying him. You sent me into hospital and they made me lay still. . . ."

The woman's voice was a background to his thoughts.

"He don't make nothing of his tumbles. Falls down over everything, our Teddy but he only laughs it off. Keeps us all in stitches."

Esmond was tapping the boy's knees with the reflex hammer and Francesca thought what good hands he had. The white cuffs were immaculate under the dark sleeves of his jacket and his signet ring gleamed gold. His face was intent and very serious. His mouth had a sensuous look and she wondered suddenly what it would be like to be kissed by him . . . shied away from the idea in a startled fashion. She was getting too emotionally involved with him and far too settled down in Regent House. It was time to move on. Nothing was worth the pain of betrayal. He looked the sort of man, who would be faithful all his life to the woman he loved . . . the beautiful Sheelagh Ross.

"The only reflexes I can get are the ankle and biceps. All the others are absent."

He was examining the boy's back, testing the strength of the various groups of muscles and in a little while, he straightened up.

"I see no possible reason to disagree with your diagnosis, Francesca."

She had gone over to pick mint sweets from the jar and she came back to give them to Teddy.

"That's all then. Away into the kitchen to Connie and tell her to find you some chocolate cake. I know it's your favourite."

Esmond had put his hand on Mrs. Graves's arm to keep her back and she turned and looked at him, when the boy had gone.

"Is it anything bad, sir?"

"We both agree that he has some trouble in

the muscles. We'll see what they think at the hospital. . . ."

"Would he get treatment there?"

"Something to strengthen the muscles perhaps."

As she listened to his pleasant voice, she thought that one did not tell mothers that there was no hope for an only child . . . no treatment . . . no future.

"He won't be a cripple, will he?"

"I don't think we should begin to worry about such a possibility, Mrs. Graves, but we should tell them at school that Teddy topples easily and they mustn't be rough with him. We don't want too much unnecessary falling about. The children will play the game if it's explained to them. They all love him . . . he's such a good chap."

"But I can't help worrying, sir. I suppose I'm the worrying kind."

"Why not have another baby, Mrs. Graves . . . get your mind of this problem?" Francesca smiled and saw Esmond's eyebrows go up.

"It's not possible," he said shortly. "There had to be a hysterectomy an hour after Teddy was born. It was a very difficult confinement."

She laughed that off and only Esmond recognised the brittle quality of her mirth.

"So you can't have any more children to worry about? You'll just have to concentrate on Whiskers then, won't you . . . and what you'll do if he brings you home another rat?"

She sat down and put her head in her hands, when the woman had gone.

"I don't know why I did medicine," she grumbled. "Murdo was against it . . . said that a woman shouldn't have to face the things we meet in the profession. Being Murdo, he maintained that men shouldn't have to face such tragedies either, but somebody has to face them."

"You've got to detach yourself, Francesca... not think of Teddy Graves as anything but an overweight, male child with reflexes absent, with hypertrophy of the calves, with this, with that. . . ."

She did not raise her head and her voice was so low, that he could scarcely hear what she said.

"That's what they teach us, isn't it? Don't think of Ted Graves and his wife in the empty house, when Teddy is dead . . . forget the way he gets knocked over at school . . . the way he gets up again with bruised knees, laughing at his own clumsiness. I know well that the only chance of survival in the torture of clinical medicine is detachment. It's the price of being the beloved physician . . . the family doctor, but what if one can't detach oneself? Oh, God blast medicine to hell!"

He put out a finger to touch her hair. It was as soft as silk and very shining. His hand went down to hold her chin and turn up her face to look at him, as he might have done to a child

"Don't take it so hard," he said gently. "Besides what would the learned gentleman from Oxford have to say to such unsuitable language?"

She smiled at him and he let his hand fall from her face.

"Actually he taught me to do it, sir. He always held that it was best to let rip with a good round oath, than to have a paralytic stroke . . .and fall dead at your own feet."

For a moment it had looked as if he meant to kiss her . . . to comfort her. She had been disappointed, that he didn't. She had never felt like this about any man but one. She had not been in his house for two months and she wanted this rather sophisticated man to kiss her. She had started to have a series of disturbing dreams about him too and she knew well that the time had come to move on again. As soon as Pat's half-term holiday was over, she would tell him she wanted to go. . . .

"The healing of the sick is an absurd form of employment," he was saying gravely. "Only think of these three cases of yours this morning . . . Miss Moss and her deaf aid . . . Billy Binns and his impetigo . . . all very well, but then we get Teddy Graves . . . a very small boy, with no future. . . ."

He shook his head at her and smiled suddenly as he went on.

"Do you know that I think it's the gentlemen, who put their nose pickings in the waste paper basket, who restore one's sense of proportion . . . make it possible to practice medicine in the first place?"

About noon on the following Thursday, Esmond Ross turned the Austin into the drive of St. Catherine's School for Young Gentlewomen and listened to an ex-pupil's candid opinion of the establishment, as he drove through the lovely park to pull up before the front door of Chaucer House.

"Chaucer was my house too and it's the best one," Francesca was saying. "It's centrally heated and the studies are good. Shakespeare's falling to bits. There's a rumour it's not safe and may fall down at any moment. Milton is for the babies . . . the under-thirteens, to you . . . and John Donne has a paranoidal maniac of a housemistress. At least in Chaucer, 'the Bun' is fairly sane."

"Miss Bunberry to me, I presume."

She looked sideways at him and thought how pleasant a companion he was . . . very attractive too in his tweed suit. He looked more relaxed than his usual self in formal town clothes.

"There's only one real snag in Chaucer and that's 'Scotty,' the matron. She doles out two cascaras every Friday night, which is deplorable from a medical point of view . . . and apart from that, there is a limit to the toilet facilities on Saturrday mornings. . . ."

"Francesca!" he laughed. "Please desist from this train of thought. Here we are at Chaucer now and we might come face to face with any member of the staff at any moment. It's sobering though to know the return one gets for the incredible fees they charge. . . ."

Pat must have been watching for them from a window, for she came running down the steps, as they pulled up.

"Oh, Daddy! It's so nice of you to have come all the way to bring me home . . . marvellous to have thought of asking for me to get away on Thursday too . . . a whole extra day."

He looked at Francesca and his eyebrows shot up, but that lady avoided his eye, as Pat hurled herself into her father's arms and murmured that it had been a wonderful scheme.

"Murdo never thought that one up for me, worse luck."

Ross introduced his daughter rather stiffly, but there was no hope of the atmosphere remaining formal.

"Oh, Frankie! I know I've never actually met you, but I feel we're old friends . . . all those letters and the cakes too. You have no idea how welcome they were."

He was lifting his brows again at his lady assistant, but she only smiled at Pat.

"Don't forget I was at Chaucer too, Mistress Pat . . . and now climb into the front of the car, for your father will want you near him and you'll have a deal to talk about. I must pay my respects to the staff. I don't know if they'll approve of my kit. Still perhaps they'll realise that what one wears on 'the boundless sea' is a far cry from academic dress."

She went up the steps of Chaucer House in one bound, her figure slim and boyish in drill slacks and a green high-necked sweater, as Esmond echoed, "The boundless sea?"

"Oh, Daddy, you know," laughed Patricia. " '*Cras ingens interabimus aequor*' . . . the school motto . . . 'tomorrow we set sail on the boundless sea'."

They got into the car and he ran his arm along the seat at her back and felt the tenderness rise in his heart at the thought of having her near him again. Francesca had talked so much of her that she had never been far from his mind. Simon had come down from the back seat too and was making a fuss of her and the time passed very pleasantly, till his assistant made her appearance again, and climbed into the rear seat to take the cat in her arms.

Esmond was disappointed not to have her beside him. As they drove towards Oxford, he contented himself with watching her reflection in the mirror. In ten minutes, he stopped the car to let Pat get out to cut some hedge plant, that she wanted for her botany class and he leaned over to talk to her and got a

149

close up view of her face. Her eyes were as green as the Hebridean seas, just as Murdo had described them, and they had little dark flecks round the iris. He had noticed the flecks the night before when he had given an anaesthetic for her to deliver the Robinson baby. She had been so intent on the job in hand that he had had the opportunity to study her at close quarters. He looked down at her slightly sulky mouth now and knew that he would have given much to take her in his arms and kiss her and that was an admission to make, even to himself. He had thought he could never love another woman and here he was, head over heels in love with this one, who was far too young for a widower in his early forties. He knew that he would ask her to marry him, given the slightest chance to think she might say yes.

"Murdo will have tinned grapefruit for lunch," she was saying. "Then peas and chips and chicken pie . . . followed by ice-cream and hot chocolate sauce. Then we'll have strong coffee made in a Cona, which I must make, but Murdo will spike it . . . spike it well too, with brandy. I'm very sorry, but it's traditional at half-term. He won't have forgotten. He'd have it for Pat, in any case,

150

because she'll love it. He loves to pander to people's tastes . . . always did. It horrifies me now, when I think of the sufferings I must have inflicted on his ageing stomach. . . ."

He got a pang of pain at the thought of Murdo's "ageing stomach." She would think him far too old to consider marrying him. He started the car abruptly, when Pat got in and sulked with her for ten minutes and she noticed it too and wondered what had upset him. She stretched her arm across his shoulder to point away to the right.

"There's our first sight of Oxford. If you have a pair of binoculars, you can see a tower, that's opposite the flat. We always stopped here, so that I got my first view of home and Murdo never forgot the glasses."

She left her hand on his shoulder in a most unselfconscious way and he stopped sulking to wonder what she would do, if he picked it up to lay it against his face. She was excited at the prospect of seeing her guardian again. When he drew up in front of the building where the flat was, she was out of the car in a flash.

"Wait here for a moment. I'll bring him down."

Murdo was at his desk in the study and he

stood up quickly and held out his hands to her. She twined her arms about his neck and kissed him warmly and his voice was thick with emotion at her obvious joy in seeing him again.

"Trews, Eh? Surely King Cophetua is not letting you wear the trews?"

"Don't dare let him know I call him that. He's downstairs in the car with Pat. I was rude, I'm afraid. I couldn't wait to see you. We must go down. . . ."

"Let them bide a wee. Tell me how you like Regent House."

"I adore it."

"And His Majesty?"

"I adore him too."

"And the vaccination? Is the immunity still holding?"

"I think so . . . perhaps not. Maybe I'll be back to this flat sooner than you think."

He put his arm round her shoulders and gave her a little shake.

"Don't be a coward, lassie. You've always run away from it. Why don't you stand and fight . . . just this once . . . to please me?"

She looked at him doubtfully.

"Is it His Majesty?"

"Don't ask me that . . . not yet. Oh, by the

way, before he . . . they come in, I must have some advice. I'll get no chance to talk to you later."

She put a hand into her pocket and took out an envelope addressed in childish block letters.

DR. FRANCESCA CUNNINGHAM,
REGENT HOUSE,
HARTON.

"It came by the post the other day."

He opened it and glanced quickly through the contents.

"Nasty dirty thing! Put it behind the fire and don't open any more, if they come. What did His Majesty have to say to it?"

She studied the carpet at her feet and her cheeks flushed a little.

"I haven't shown it to him. I couldn't let him see that sort of stuff."

"Put it away for now then, but he'll have to see it later. We'll get Mistress Patricia out of the way first. As like as not, he's had one of the things himself, and it's best to get the like of yon out into the fresh air."

They showed him the letter after lunch and the meal had been exactly as Francesca had foretold, down to what Esmond described as brandy spiked with coffee, which Pat sipped appreciatively, remarking,

"I don't know what they'd say at St. Catherine's."

"Well your matron couldn't object," Murdo remarked gloomily. "She's ruining the bowels of hundreds of potential mothers with her blasted cascara on Friday nights. Never swallow them, Mistress Pat. Even if the taste kills you, just you hold them in your mouth and spit them down the privy, when you get the chance. If the good Lord wanted that sort of thing, he'd have seen fit to build in a gland to manufacture cascara every seven days. Who is this 'Scotty,' may I inquire, that she dares to tamper with the handiwork of the Almighty?"

He looked across smouldering at Esmond and saw the disapproval in his eyes at such conversation and was driven to continue.

"Besides, they'd want to treble the amount of heads, if they plan to carry out that type of mass evacuation. . . ."

He sent Patricia off to buy herself a box of chocolates and to do several other small messages for him that would keep her away for half an hour and when she had gone, he stretched out his hand to Francesca.

"Now, lassie, out with it!"

She looked at him appealingly and then bent her head to look at the floor at her feet.

"I'd rather not."

He put out his hand again and picked the letter out of her pocket.

"My lassie is ashamed to show you this, Esmond, and she's been worried out of wits about it too. I told her it's quite likely that you might have had one as well and it's best discussed between us."

The letter was almost identical to the one that Piggott had brought to the surgery. Esmond's eyes went down the cut-out print, gummed to cheap paper.

"Dear Miss Cunningham,

You're not liked in Harton and you'd better get out. The decent married women will put you in the pond and drown you, if you don't go. You may think you're beautiful, but as a jewel in a pig's snout, so is a fair woman without discretion. You dirty rotten little . . ."

Esmond's face flushed as he read to the end

of the letter. Then he glanced over towards her downbent head.

"I'm sorry you've had one of these. Ron Piggott brought a similar document up to my surgery recently and I thought there'd be more of them. I had one today myself, before we left and I wouldn't have believed how upsetting it can be."

He took an envelope from his jacket and passed it to his friend.

"I'd prefer that Francesca didn't see it."

Murdo drew his black brows into a scowl and remarked that his ward was no hot-house lily and then he turned his attention to the letter.

"Dear Dr. Ross,

How hast thou fallen, from heaven, O Lucifer, son of the morning! Your new lady may be very beautiful when she's in her own bed, but at the times, when I stand in your drive . . ."

"And signed 'a Patient,' " he grunted and threw it down on the table beside Francesca.

"Read it child. It's a medical item of interest . . . the result of a diseased mind. My

156

bet is that it's written by a female . . .
frustrated too . . . always is."

She picked it up doubtfully and her eyes
went to Esmond.

"If you'd prefer me not to . . ."

"Please yourself," he said shortly and
wheeled away to stand at the window with his
back to the room.

She dropped her gaze to the letter and felt a
little sick at the thought that some person
possessed enough hate towards her to con-
trive such a letter. She put up a hand to her
forehead to hide the tide of colour that
flooded her cheeks and knew that he had been
right not to want her to see such disgusting
sentences and words and expressions.

"Was Piggott's letter about me too?"

He turned back from the window to look at
her and felt fury at the writer of the letter,
when he saw the down-bent head.

"Good Lord, no! It was about an unspeci-
fied woman. It accused Piggott of gross
immorality in pretty horrible terms too, but
no name was mentioned. The words were cut
from print and the notepaper was the same
cheap stuff. I think we should burn all the
letters forthwith and try to put the matter out
of our minds."

Murdo shook his head doubtfully and suggested that that was the worst possible course of action.

"You'll have to put them in the hands of the police and there's no escape from it. It's a filthy business and it'll start everybody looking over their shoulders . . . saying 'Is it she . . . or maybe she . . . or maybe he?' Let's try to face it. It's someone who knows the household. I suppose I'm not in the running, or Pat for that matter, unless we could find a method of posting the damn things in Harton, for the post mark is the same on each envelope. It might be either of you two, or Connie, or that good nurse from Wales. It's got to be thrashed out and the finger put on the felon. Without that, there's going to be mischief. Look at my lassie there and how upset she is. You'd find her packing her bags one morning, my friend, to get out of the atmosphere of the place."

"That's ridiculous, Murdo," she said. "I'm not going to leave Harton . . . certainly not on account of a few stupid letters. I'm certainly not convinced of any danger in all those warnings. . . ."

Before the words were out of her mouth, she wondered what had made her say she was not going to leave Regent House. She had already decided that she must go, though for a very different reason. She knew with a sinking of her heart that she was in love with Esmond Ross . . . and she was a fool. She hadn't got out in time. She should have gone the moment she had stood on the platform at Wentbridge and put her hand in his. It was far too late to run now. She thought ruefully that she had no choice but to take her guardian's advice to stand and fight. The immunity, of which she was so certain, had failed and she was facing the agony of a broken heart all over again. There was no possible chance of him falling in love with Francesca Cunningham . . . not after having possessed the beautiful Sheelagh Ross, who still haunted all the dark remembered corridors of his mind. She was a fool . . . a stupid blundering fool . . . and that was all there was to it.

It was not long before the next poison pen letters came to light. The half-term week-end had passed off very successfully and Pat had gone back to school. Connie had been subdued for the next few days, but Francesca had thought it was because she was lonely for Pat.

It was not for almost a week, when she began to wonder if there was not a more sinister explanation for the white face and the troubled eyes. Then one morning, she surprised the housekeeper in the kitchen with another of the by now familiar letters in her hand.

"I thought so, Mistress Constance. Why on earth didn't you tell us about it? I've had one of these myself. . . ."

She read the crudely cut-out words, that made up the text . . .

"Dear Madam,
I do not know if you are aware of the fact that you're living in a house of wickedness and that the bitch you think of as Dr. Cunningham has come from a house of incest to . . ."

"More quotations from the scriptures . . . 'Oh, generation of vipers, who hath warned you to flee from the wrath to come?' signed 'a Well-wisher' too. My, oh, my!"

"God above, Doctor!" wept Connie. "Who would make out a thing the like of that?"

Francesca made her no answer, but went out to the waiting-room, fetched Nurse

Roberts and put the letter into her hand. The nurse's face went scarlet as she read it and then she put her hand into the pocket of the apron.

"I've had one like it. It had me worried out of my mind what to do about it."

It differed only in its wording from its fellows.

"Dear Nurse Roberts,

You're in love with Esmond Ross and you old enough to be his mother, but you're done with him, for he has no eyes for an old flame, when there's a . . ."

"I don't know who wrote it, but it's a sin for them to bring a bit of the Bible into it," the nurse cried. "Look at the end of it there. 'As a dog returneth to his vomit, so a fool returneth to his folly.' 'You have been warned,' indeed! I didn't like to show it to you or the doctor. A body would be ashamed, for all that it's a pack of lies. . . ."

Francesca put both letters in the pocket of her white coat and went back to the surgeries. She tapped softly at Esmond's door, but there was no reply and she went in. He was sitting at his desk with his head in his hands, but the

161

cat saw her and jumped down from the desk to rub himself against her ankles.

"I thought there was nobody here. You didn't hear me knock."

He started a little and then stood up and walked to the fire, leaning heavily on his stick.

"I've just had Graves here . . . Teddy's father. You saw that the hospital agreed with our diagnosis, so the boy has muscular dystrophy and will go steadily downhill, till he's crippled in a year or two."

"Poor Teddy!"

"Ted asked me to give him the full picture. It wasn't very . . . pleasant. We decided to keep the mother out of it, as long as we can."

He bent down to stroke the cat, which had gone back to circulate round his ankles.

"He took it very courageously . . . said his only aim was to see that the boy packs a lifetime of happiness into what few years are left. . . . They haven't got much worldly wealth, but it's a happy house."

He straightened up and stood looking at her broodingly.

"I said what I could . . . the usual anodyne we dish out in such cases . . . there's always hope of a cure being discovered . . . the

Almighty will grant them extra strength to bear the burden . . . and talking about that, I had your friend, Zachary Monk down to see me just now too."

"You know Bill Monaghan agrees that the pregnancy should be terminated," she said. "There's no improvement after weeks of psychiatric treatment. She's acutely depressed and suicidal."

"Well, Monk is still holding out for the baby's right of eternal life. We had quite an argument about it, but who's to say my ideas are right and his are wrong?"

She went over to sit at the desk, her face grim. "So Monk is sentencing them all to a lifetime of misery on the chance of there being an eternal happiness for the child to inherit?"

"There almost certainly is such a thing," he reminded her quietly.

"And suppose there isn't? Suppose when we're dead, we're dead? Then it's all for nothing . . . all this pain and misery."

"The final choice was his and he made it, God help him! I hope Rachael doesn't kill herself one of these days. Her life must be hell. . . ."

"Life's stupid," she broke out suddenly,

laying the letters on the desk. "And there's some more stupidity for you. I know you've been very much against handing the poison pen business over to the police, but I think there's no escape from it now. It's gone on far too long as it is."

He read the letters with distaste and then looked at her reflectively.

"Monk knows his Bible from cover to cover and there's a deal of the scriptures about these . . . and the others too. He disapproves of you for that matter, though I can't see him doing such mischief. Still I agree, it's time we called a halt to it."

Sergeant Bullen had not dealt with the case himself. He came down straight away and heard what they had to say and then he read the letters for himself and grumbled at the doctors for not reporting the matter sooner. He stood in the surgery with his back to the fire, wondering if Dr. Cunningham could be responsible for writing the letters. They had started after her arrival and she certainly had a prominent place in the filthy subject matter they contained. She might be trying to draw attention to herself . . . yet she did not look the type.

She caught him watching her and read his thoughts with an accuracy, that embarrassed him.

"Don't look at me like that. I never done it, Sergeant."

He looked down at the toes of his highly-polished shoes and his face flushed.

"I wasn't thinking you did, Doctor. I was figuring out that I'll have to call headquarters about this. Inspector Taylor will likely take it over personally. He's hot on this sort of thing. He'll get the blokes at Castle Hill working on it. I'll ring you presently and arrange when we can interview you both. . . ."

He arrived back at Regent House after lunch, accompanied by Inspector Percy Taylor and Detective Constable Hacker, and Connie showed them into the sitting-room. It was the first time Francesca had seen Taylor and she looked up at him as he shook hands with her and thought she had never seen such an enormous man before. He was six foot three at a rough estimate and very powerfully built, not the traditional police inspector, but far more like a company director out for a day at Newmarket, in his well-cut suit and good tie. Yet he proved himself to be all policeman in the first five minutes. He stood at

Esmond's table desk and laid the letters out in a row on the red top.

"I've had time to take a look at these. Pretty, aren't they?"

His voice was incisive, pleasant, clipped, with rather a nasal quality about it.

"There's something here, that gives a clue to one of the newspapers used. See . . . 'At the times, when I stand in your drive . . .' "

He put his thumb nail under the line and Bullen stood at his side and bent his head down.

"See anything, Bullen?"

"It's not cut tidily, sir. It actually reads 'at the Times Pub when I stand. . . .' "

Taylor had wheeled about on Hacker, who was trying to make himself unobtrusive by the window.

"Does that suggest anything to you, boy?"

There was a whiplash quality about his voice that made the unfortunate Hacker spring to attention.

"I don't know any pub of that name, sir."

"Good grief, Hacker! Can you never get your mind off beer?"

Taylor picked up a copy of *The Times* from one of the chairs and turned it over to the back page.

"Do you mind if I mutilate your paper, sir?" he asked Esmond and took a small silver penknife out of his pocket.

"The Times Publishing Company," he murmured and cut out a tiny scrap of newsprint, laid it down triumphantly on the white blotter.

"Now you see it. Now you don't! And who in the village of Harton has *The Times* delivered regularly, Bullen?"

"They take it at the Grange, sir . . . and they have it here. I should think that's about all. If Dr. Ross'll let me use the phone, I'll ring them at the Post Office Stores and find out."

The inspector shot a sarcastic look at his constable.

"Let Hacker do it. At least he'll be able to use the telephone, when he's through his training. God knows he'll have to have something to show for it."

The constable made for the door, walking on tiptoe, to try to minimise the effect of his heavy boots and Francesca looked reprovingly at Taylor.

"You shouldn't be so hard on him, Inspector. We've all got to learn."

167

His moustache went up under his nose in a genial smile.

"Only way to train 'em, lady. You mightn't think it to look at him, but Hacker is the most promising lad I've had through my hands for years. I'll make a detective of him yet."

"I think you're far more likely to break his heart."

He shot up an eyebrow to look at her, askance.

"I don't break their hearts, Dr. Cunningham. I'll leave that to you."

He liked her at once. Bullen had told him that she seemed honest and forthright, but she seemed to be the centre of the whole rotten affair, except for Piggott's letter, which was odd man out. Whoever had written the things had it in for her. There was no doubt about that . . . and Ross was obviously taken with her . . . couldn't keep his eyes off her for two minutes running. She was a damned attractive girl too, with her dimples winking in and out all the time. Break Hacker's heart indeed! He looked to see what colour her eyes were and saw they were dark green. Pity they weren't brown. Peg, his wife had brown eyes and Peg was a beautiful woman . . . different from this one

168

though . . . classic, white-skinned. Dr. Cunningham had a face the colour of a peach . . . an impish peach. What a description! It was a good thing Ross couldn't read his thoughts. He'd marry his lady within a twelve month and good luck to him! They said he was a broken man after that other affair, but he must have picked up the pieces by this.

Hacker was in the room and was looking at him like a terrier looking for a bone.

"There's only two copies of *The Times* delivered in the village sir, one to the Grange and one here."

Francesca was smiling at Bullen now.

"I'm getting in pretty deep, Sergeant, but I still maintain I never done it."

Bullen was getting hot under the collar and the inspector wondered what was the matter with him. There was some private joke between him and the lady doctor, but he'd break it up sharp like.

"There must be more copies of *The Times* knocking about, Bullen. Anyone can go into Wentbridge and buy one. There'll be more of these letters too. Get cracking on it. I want some more of the damned things . . . and I want them soon. Check with the dust men for cut-up newsprint . . . burnt paper . . . the usual drill."

He swept the letters up into his hand and gave them to Hacker.

"See anything else, boy? It's sticking out a mile."

The constable's voice broke with nervousness.

"I did notice the texts, sir . . . from the Bible, sir, but I didn't like to say anything. . . ."

"Didn't like to say anything. Haven't you got a tongue in your head? What do you think it's for? Come on, out with it! What have we all missed?"

"I know you didn't miss it, sir. You never miss nothing, but it's these texts. They're not cut out of a paper, sir. I'd say they're out of a Bible. There's no division between the words. Look here in this one. 'How art thou fallen from heaven, O Lucifer, son of the morning.' It's in two lines and the print is big. It might be an old family Bible, sir. You often see them still."

Francesca looked sideways at the sergeant and smiled.

"That lets me out, Sergeant Bullen. I haven't got one of those."

"Perhaps I'll not want your fingerprints after all then, Doctor."

The inspector had taken the letters back from Hacker to spread them on the desk top again.

"You're sure all those texts are from the Bible, boy? Even that one about the pig's snout? It doesn't sound like the Bible to me."

"It's out of Proverbs, sir. So is the one about the dog and the vomit."

"Well, I'll go to sea!"

"You seem to be very familiar with the scriptures, Constable Hacker," Esmond observed and the man nodded his head.

"My old mother was a rare one for religion, sir. We lived in a cottage on the river . . . Upware way. Ten of us, and she had us at Bible reading Sundays. Chapter turn about, we'd read and we'd be at it all the afternoon and then she'd pray over us. My dad would want to go fishing, but she'd have none of that on the Lord's Day, and he'd have to stay and read his chapter, when his turn came. I remember one day, I got the 119th Psalm and I said I had the belly-ache. Cor! She raised blisters on me with the copper stick."

Inspector Taylor stuck his hands in his

jacket pockets and looked at his officer with amazement.

"And what's wrong with the 119th Psalm, boy?"

"It's on the long side, sir."

"Your tongue is on the long side too, Hacker. Still, it shows you can use every bit of knowledge you possess. Only for Hacker's mother now, we wouldn't have known that bit about Proverbs. I suppose we'd better look out for a family Bible then."

"There's a big Bible at the Grange, sir," Bullen put in. "Stands in the sitting-room on a table, but there's plenty more about the village."

"Who lives at the Grange besides Mrs. Mallory and her grand-nephew?"

"Ellen and James Ferguson, sir . . . house-keeper and butler, and two girls called Goodge, but they go home at night."

The inspector was looking down at the letters.

"Cheap notepaper . . . cheap envelopes to match. Check samples at the shops in the village. Check for sales of bottles of gum. The writing might have been done by a child, but this is no child's work . . . written in aqua-marine ink with a ball point pen. Check sales

172

of ball point pens. The tone of the letter is that of an educated person . . . a bit cracked, or more than a bit. Get out a list of probables, Hacker. There's a deal of dirt aimed at our lady here . . . and the writer knew she lived in Oxford. I imagine that the Goodge girls are out for a start. They'd not write things like 'House of wickedness' or 'House of incest.' ''

Francesca bit her under lip and looked at him demurely.

"Besides which, they wouldn't have taught them how to spell some of those words in the village school."

Ross was put out by her frivolity.

"Is everything always so funny to you, Francesca?"

"Not always, but quite often. It's one method of not losing one's sense of proportion, I suppose. . . .''

"And I like to hear the lady's views," Taylor put in. "She's got a refreshing approach to crime . . . and she's right about the spelling for that matter. It certainly wasn't learnt in Harton School and that lets out a great number of people, who might be suspect."

She pushed her hands deep into the pockets of her skirt and glanced over at Esmond.

"You were right too. There isn't anything funny about any part of it. You know there are two copies of *The Times* delivered locally and your mind focuses down to actual people . . . the Mallorys, the Fergusons, Connie, Nurse Roberts. It all becomes personal then and it's not an abstruse hypothetical problem any more. I'm frightened. I'm whistling in the dark, Ess-mond. . . ."

The "Esmond" slipped out of her mouth before she could stop it and, of course, he noticed it. She was awkward in a flash and bent her head to hide her embarrassment, not meeting his eye.

"I'm sorry, Dr. Ross. I've no right to use your first name. It was hearing Murdo doing it all the time. I do apologise about it. I deserve 'Murdo's judgement' for my impertinence. Truly I do."

"It's quite permissible to use my Christian name. I don't remember asking if I might use yours. Besides you always call the First Gentleman, Murdo. It's much more pleasant between friends."

It seemed to Percy Taylor that these two moved in a magic world of their own . . . a thing of great beauty and worth. Ross was smiling at her and love for her was written

174

plainly in his face, if she would only look at him.

"I'd not dream of submitting you to your guardian's judgement for such a small slip of the tongue."

She was still flushed as she thanked him . . . still slightly awkward with him and Taylor wondered who the First Gentleman was, and what her guardian's judgement might be, when it was at home.

"So I'm to have an amnesty then, Essmond . . . like the small gentleman with the tail? I thank you."

For God's sake, thought the Inspector, we are acting Romeo and Juliet . . . and who or what was "the small gentleman with the tail?" Oh well, he would let them get on with it. He swept all the letters up from the desk again and cleared his throat.

"Well, we'll be getting along then. We've made a start and thank you both for your co-operation. If any more letters come in, perhaps you'd handle them as little as possible and let me have them unopened. That way, we might get prints. . . ."

In the weeks before Easter, Esmond Ross seemed to himself to inhabit some secret land

175

of magic with his lady . . . magic, that increased as they got to know each other more and more. Taylor had been right about that, for he was a shrewd judge of human relationships. Esmond grew more and more enchanted with her and he found himself listening to hear her call him by name. She said it in a characteristic way, rather sibilantly . . . "Ess-mond" . . . with a little pause between the syllables. Sometimes he surprised a warm look in her eyes, or caught her watching him covertly and he began to hope that she loved him too. He had almost got up his courage to ask her to marry him, when he caught a chill. She insisted on calling Don Jones out to see him and that gentleman found a patch of congestion in one lung and confined him to bed for a fortnight.

She went up to his room to discuss the calls the first morning, very unself-conscious about seeing him in his bed. She wandered in and out of his bathroom and dressing-room very casually, talking shop all the time.

"There's a visit to the Grange to see Miss Mallory, Ess-mond. I'll meet Lucien at last and be able to decide for myself, if he's as attractive as all the ladies think."

He remarked testily that, to his mind,

176

Lucien Mallory was an excellent example of the havoc that the skin disease known as Common Acne, could cause on the human face, and she grinned at him like a school boy.

"Acne Vulgaris? Then he'll be rugged-looking and manly. I hope I'm smartly enough dressed for the visit."

He was put out by her interest in Mallory and he frowned at her as she stood at the foot of the bed. She was wearing a skirt of almost white tweed and her green roll-necked jumper and he thought the light coloured tweed made her very dark and attractive. It was a shock to him to realise that the bitter feeling in his chest could only be diagnosed as jealousy.

"Don't take Mallory too lightly. It's possible that he may be one of those subjects you can't joke about. He has a bad reputation, you know."

"Oh, come now, Ess-mond. You don't think I'd ever get serious about Mr. Acne Vulgaris? I'd never be able to marry him, knowing that you'd think of me as Mrs. Vulgaris . . . even Lady Vulgaris of The Grange. Oh, no! He's not for me."

"I hope you get on amicably with his grand-aunt then. I'm afraid she may be a little difficult with you. She was very angry with me for taking in a lady assistant. Perhaps you had better go there first and get it over. She's ill too . . . heart in failure. The devil is that she'll never listen to advice. She's as stubborn as a mule. I'm sorry you've had to visit her in the first place."

She was leaving for her call at the Grange, when the emergency came in. Connie ran down the hall to stop her, as she opened the car door.

"Oh, God! I thought I'd missed you. There's been a phone call. Rachael Monk's gassed herself. Will you go at once, Doctor . . . the cottage in Pepys Close . . . as quickly as you can. They think she's dead. . . ."

She forced herself to think calmly, though her heart had started to thump like a sledge hammer. The emergency bag was in the boot and she shifted it to the back seat.

"Ring the ambulance, Connie. Tell them what's happened. Say we'll want the oxygen kit."

She drove very quickly through the village with the thoughts rocketing round in her head. Of course, the girl had killed herself. People said that a patient never committed suicide, if they threatened to do it beforehand, but that was nonsense . . . had been proved untrue time and again. How could her parents watch her every hour of the day? What was the use of limiting the supply of tablets, with the gas tap ready to her hand? The level crossing gates were just closing and she kept her thumb on the horn desperately. The porter took one look at the car and opened them back and she bumped over the rails. She pulled to a halt outside the Monks' cottage in another minute, praying that somebody had had the common sense to pull the girl's body out into the fresh air . . . to start respiration, no matter how dead she looked. The reek of gas met her, as she tore down the side passage and came on a group of people at the back door, and there was Rachael, lying on the ground, a pillow under her head and a rug thrown over her. Mrs. Monk was weeping in the arms of a neighbour.

"She's dead, Doctor. You're too late. She's killed herself. My Rachael has killed herself. She said she'd do it, and none of us believed her. . . ."

The girl did not look dead. The gas poisoning had given a flush to her cheeks, but she had stopped breathing. Francesca put the tip of the stethoscope down on to the chest wall and heard nothing but the blood pounding in her own ears . . . and Mrs. Monk's voice wailed loudly as a background.

"Be quiet. I can't hear, if you make that noise."

She bent her head to listen again and heard the neighbour's voice.

"Hush, now, dear. She's trying to help Rachael, but you must be quiet. . . ."

The lub-dub of the heart was so faint as to be almost imagined, but it was there. She rolled the girl on her face and knelt on the ground beside her and the air rushed out of the lungs, as she pressed down hard with both hands.

"Will she be all right, miss?" a woman asked and Francesca looked up at her.

"I don't know, I hope so. Get a rag and keep her mouth clear. . . ."

The sweat was running down her forehead into her eyes after three minutes of it and her own breath was panting, as if she had run a race. She shrugged out of her jacket and went on grimly, knowing that no matter how quickly the ambulance came, it would seem like a thousand years. She stopped for a moment to feel the pulse and it was just perceptible and she felt encouraged as she went on doggedly with the rhythmic movements . . . press . . . pause . . . release . . . press . . . pause . . . release.

There was a squeal of brakes, and boots, that clattered up the flagged path and Sergeant Bullen was there with Bob Tanner at his heels. Tanner knelt down and took over the artificial respiration without a word and she stood up and smiled wearily at Bullen.

"Thank God you're here. It's a lonely feeling. . . ."

Another five minutes, and Bullen had relieved Tanner. Rachael was beginning to snore in the back of her throat, and now and again, she moaned slightly. Then all at once, the ambulance was there, the ting-ting-ting of its bell, louder and louder, and again the clattering of men's boots on the path and the two blue-uniformed men at her side. She thought back to the night she had told Nigel they were all one big team and knew how true her words had been. She knew the fair-haired ambulance man as Harry . . . knew he was a judo expert. He had the oxygen mask on Rachael's face in ten seconds. They were miracles of efficiency, these men. In no time at all, they were loading the girl into the back of the ambulance. She was sobbing into the mask now and Harry was stooping down to talk to her.

"There, there, miss! You'll be all right. There's nothing to cry about."

"That's the understatement of all time," Bullen's voice murmured in her ear. "Poor little devil! Of all the girls in the county, she deserved it the least."

She watched the ambulance reverse slowly along the narrow road, to turn at the far end and head for Wentbridge, its blue light flashing and its alarm tinging. Then she walked slowly back along the flags of the path and Bullen put the suicide note into her hand . . . the usual heart-broken pathetic farewell to her loved ones . . . and down almost at the end of it ". . . I know, Dad, you've always taught me that the wages of sin is death. . . ."

"It was on the mantelpiece and she had a photograph of her mum and dad by her hand. . . ."

Of course, Bullen was on to the Biblical quotation, like a cat pouncing on a mouse.

"That's from the scriptures, isn't it? 'The wages of sin is death?' I wonder. . . . Still I hardly think. . . . It's an open and shut case of attempted suicide at any rate. Her head was on a pillow in the oven and the doors and windows were sealed up with rugs and blankets. I'll have to send in a report to headquarters. . . ."

She got away at last and went back to Nurse Roberts' house to wash and tidy herself. Then she returned to Regent House, to tell Esmond what had happened. They rang the hospital and found that Rachael had arrived safely and was doing as well as could be expected.

She felt exhausted, mentally and physically as she got into the car to start her rounds. On the short drive to the Grange, she told herself that it was no use being dispirited, for there was a great deal of work to be done. She pulled herself together, as she went up the front steps of the old house to knock at the gigantic knocker. The sound echoed in a ghostly way and after a long time, a white-haired old man opened the door, with surprise in his faded blue eyes at the sight of her.

"I'm Dr. Cunningham. I've come to see Miss Mallory. Dr. Ross is ill and a request for a visit came in this morning. I'm standing in for him."

He opened the door more widely to let her come into the hall, but his face was doubtful.

"I'll have to ask, madam, I don't know what the mistress will say. Will you take a seat for a moment? I'll go and inquire. . . ."

He went off along the hall like an old tortoise, his head bent forward, and she saw him mounting the stairs at the far end. This was a nice state of affairs, she thought, putting her case down on the hall chair and walking up and down the flagged floor impatiently. The place was cold and dank and smelt musty. You could see the grooves that had been worn by generations of feet, passing to the dining-room on the left and the drawing-room on the right. There was a dark oak chest along one wall, that was large enough to contain ten corpses, Francesca thought, as she shivered in the draught that was coming in under the front door.

A riding mackintosh had been thrown down on one of the chairs in the sitting-room with its red lining outwards, and on the floor beneath was a hunting crop. They would belong to Lucien. The furniture was hall-marked as Victorian by the bobbles along the red velvet, that draped the mantelpiece, and the great gold mirror above, its paint chipped and cracking. The family Bible, that the police had spoken of, was on a small square table just inside the door and she wondered if she would have time to have a look at it. She glanced up the stairs, but everywhere was as silent as a tomb, so she went into the room quickly and opened back the cover of the book. It was damp-mouldy and the name was blotched.

LUCIEN THEOPHILUS MALLORY
1825

She turned a page and came on a history of the family in flowing old-fashioned characters, written in by various hands, as each event had happened. There was no time to read it properly, but she scanned down the entries.

"On November the eleventh, in the year of our Lord, 1825, at the Parish Church of Harton, my dear wife and I were wed. . . ."

Under this were details of the births and deaths of various children and she picked one out. . . .

"Died, In Harton Grange, at eight o'clock in the evening, in the year of our Lord, 1836, my dearest and eldest son, Lucien, aged ten years. His last words were 'I hear the church bell calling me. It is Jesus calling me to come to Him?' These words were spoken to my dear wife and then the boy went asleep in her arms and woke no more in this world. . . ."

Another paragraph caught her interest on the next page.

"7th day of September in the year 1850, my dear wife, Margaret Ellen Charlotte was today committed to a private lunatic asylum in Bedford. My life has ended with her departure from this house. . . ."

There was page after page of the family history, but there was no time to read it. Francesca leafed quickly over to the Book of Proverbs, but the text had not been mutilated in any way that she could see. She closed the book carefully and went out to the hall again, her nerves rather on edge, as she waited in silence. It was five minutes before anybody came and then Ellen Ferguson appeared by her side, as silently as if she had come there by magic . . . clad in a black dress and a white apron, her hands clasped in front of her, her face agitated.

"Oh, Miss Cunningham," she quavered. "Miss Mallory always has Dr. Esmond. Is he really too ill to come? Could he not get up and come to see her and then go back to bed again? Miss Mallory is very put out with him."

"He's far too ill to get up and I'm perfectly capable of attending to Miss Mallory."

"I don't know what to do, madam. I'm that worried about it. She says to tell you that Dr. Esmond must get up and come at once, because it's urgent."

"I'll go up and have a word with her about that," Francesca said grimly, picking up her bag from the chair. "I've wasted enough time here as it is. There are other patients in the village who are probably far more in need of help than Miss Mallory. Please take me to her at once."

Ellen made a feeble effort to take the case from her hand.

"I'll carry this, madam."

"Indeed, you'll do no such thing. It's far too heavy. You go ahead and show me the room."

She trudged slowly up the beautiful staircase behind Ellen's thin shanks, noticing with a smile, the white marble statues, that decorated the landings. Somebody, the patient presumably, had thought fit to drape their most intimate parts with linen cloths. Even the ladies' bosoms were covered disreetly with snow-white linen and Francesca wondered what the sculptor would have said, if he had been alive to see what had happened to his masterpieces. She was surprised that Esmond had not told her about it. Perhaps he had not thought it a fitting subject to discuss with a woman, even a medical colleague? Ellen was opening a door on the first floor landing, her voice more tremulous than ever.

"I'm sorry, madam, but Dr. Esmond is really too ill to come, and this is his lady."

Francesca walked over to the foot of the four-poster bed, prepared to do battle. She looked down on a most beautiful, white-haired old lady, whose violet shawl matched a pair of brilliant violet eyes, matched the violet silk ribbons on two snow-white plaits. The sunlight was pouring through a big window to wink and sparkle on the massed diamond rings on her arthritic fingers.

"Dr. Esmond can't be ill," Miss Mallory declared in an autocratic deep voice. "He's never ill. You run away, young lady, and tell him to get up and come here at once. His father never behaved in such a stupid way, taking to his bed and hiding behind a gel's skirts."

"He really is very ill," Francesca smiled and forced herself to remember the statues on the stairs in an effort to retain her rising temper.

"I don't want a woman doctor. I knew this was what would happen the moment he took up with you. He had no right to do it when I raised such an objection. My father employed his father and his father before him. His family has always attended ours and I'm not going to put up with it. Young people have no thought for anybody but themselves nowadays."

"You're not having much thought for anybody but yourself at this moment," Francesca reminded her quietly.

"How dare you say that to me? I don't approve of ladies in the medical profession. In my day, no lady would have stooped to it. My father was an admiral."

Francesca's hands went deep into her pockets.

"I don't care if your father was God Almighty. I have a village of sick people waiting for my help. I'm a qualified doctor. I have no particular desire to examine you, or have anything whatever to do with you. You're just another job of work to me. Whether you're the Colonel's Lady, or Judy O'Grady isn't important . . . at any rate not to me. What is important is that you're ill and you want help. If you do want *my* help, just say so. If you don't, tell me to get to hell out of here. Just make up your mind."

The old woman jerked herself upright.

"Whose father?" she screeched. "Whose father did you say you didn't care was mine?"

"I said, 'God Almighty's' but if that offends you, you can substitute the Shah of Persia or the Emperor of China. He's your father . . . not mine."

"That's blasphemy, what you said. . . ."

She sounded like a parrot and Esmond would be furious about what she had said to his best private patient.

"You deserve a whipping for blasphemy."

"Oh, for heaven's sake, who's going to whip me? Mr. Acne Vulgaris? Your great-nephew? From what I hear, ma'am, he dissipates his energies. Let him stick to his horses . . . or his women, but not both. He hasn't the staying power."

The old lady was laughing, her face cracking open, her teeth flashing creamily . . . far too perfect to be natural.

"Esmond picked a well-plucked 'un in you," she cackled. "Tell me. Are you going to marry him?"

Francesca was taken off balance by the question and she stood biting her lip, her cheeks flushing.

"I'm going to marry nobody. I haven't the time for it. There are too many patients ill, or imagining themselves ill and too few doctors to go round . . . even lady doctors."

"It's a pity then, for if I could persuade Lucy to have you, we might breed the rotten streak out of the family. It was the first Lucy's wife brought it in and it crops up now and again. We want fresh stock. We're old and sick. . . ."

She pulled herself up short.

"What did you call Lucy? Mr. Acne something. . . ."

"I'm sorry. That was unforgiveable of me. I lost my temper. It's a skin disease that pits the face. I was told he's scarred by it, but it's no fault of his and I'm ashamed of having said that. . . ."

"So you can be humble too . . . a lass of

many parts? Would you have Lucy if he asked you?"

"I told you I'm too busy for marriage. Now, if you'd like me to examine you, let's get started. If not . . ."

"Ellen, remove my shawl. . . ."

Francesca went carefully over the chest and back, hearing the weak and irregular heart beat, the crackling like a thorn fire at the bases of the lungs.

"You haven't been taking the tablets, Dr. Ross prescribed, have you?"

"They make me get out to the commode all the time. I won't take them. It's no good him prescribing them."

Francesca touched the chest, the swollen legs, the swollen fingers, turning the rings about with difficulty.

"You'd prefer the water to lie here . . . and here . . . and here?"

She finished her examination and helped Ellen to put back the nightdress and the shawl and tuck the covers into position.

"Dr. Ross has already said what I'll say now. It's no good asking for advice and then ignoring it. Your heart is a bad pump. It's leaving you marshy. You're like the Fens, before they were drained. All we're trying to do is to flog that heart of yours to do its work."

"And what if it's a dying horse, Dr. Cunningham?" the old woman asked shrewdly.

"It *is* a dying horse. We're all dying . . . even the baby I delivered last night. Nobody gets younger. So, for Pete's sake, flog the blasted horse. At least, that way, you won't drown in the swamp . . . and that's a bad way to go."

Miss Mallory sat back and smiled complacently.

"I like you, Francesca Cunningham. I thought I wouldn't . . . but I do. You say what's in your mind and that's what I like to hear. I'll have you to attend to me for the future. You can tell your employer that he's to send you, when I request a visit. He's not one half as expert as his lady assistant. He's afraid of me, but you're not."

"Of course, he's not afraid of you. Essmond's manners are better than mine . . . that's all, but my manners are good enough, not to steal his patients. I'll be pleased to attend you till he's better. Then I'll hand you back to him . . . with thanks."

Miss Mallory had started to laugh again.

"So you call him Esmond, do you? You're

193

in love with him too. I thought that would be the way of it. Don't you know the way your eyes look, every time he's mentioned, you silly gel? I'll tell him to marry you, when he calls on me again. He'll not get another like you in a month of Sundays . . . but I'm sorry you'd not have Lucy."

Francesca gritted her teeth and turned towards the door. Then she spun on her heel and came back to the foot of the bed.

"If you dare to tell him that, I'll give you an injection of arsenic. You see if I don't!"

She went off down the stairs in a fury with Ellen trotting behind her.

"Nobody ever spoke to the mistress like that before," she bleated.

"It's high time they did."

She threw the case into the back of the car and got in behind the wheel. The M.G. was being rebored and she was driving Esmond's Vanden Plas. She banged the door shut and went off down the drive in a whirl of gravel, going far too fast in her anger, rounding the corner before the gate at a good fifty miles an hour. There was a young man on a chestnut horse right in her path. She swung the wheel hard over and skidded on the verge, cutting a great swathe in its perfection and the horse

194

reared up and made a great bound in the other direction.

"God blast you, Ross! Are you out of your mind? What the hell do you think you're doing?"

She got out of the car rather shakily, her face as white as a ghost's and looked up into the angry countenance of Mr. Acne Vulgaris. Of course, Esmond had been wrong about him. He was very attractive, with deep blue eyes and golden hair, which fell over his brow. The scarring had the effect of making him look virile and tough, and did not detract from his looks in the slightest. Her heart missed a beat at the sight of him and she felt the old pain in her breast. The horse was still jumping about the grass edging, but he controlled it easily enough.

"I'm sorry," she said in a small voice. "It's that damned grand-aunt of yours. It's no excuse for reckless driving of course, but she's a——"

"I know," he smiled. "I'm sorry for shouting at you. I thought you were Ross, but you're his lady."

"I'm not his damned lady," she said sulkily. "I don't know why everybody calls me that. I'm his damned assistant . . . and a very junior one at that. Oh, damn! Look what I've done to the verge."

He slid down from the saddle and came over to stand beside her, with the horse's reins looped over his arm.

"You're fabulous!" he remarked. "You're far more fabulous than they all say you are. I heard that you've got sparkle to you, but you've got fire."

She raised one eybrow at him whimsically and made a self-deprecating moue.

"That's uncommonly civil of you, Mr. Mallory, particularly when I've just nearly run you down with the car."

"I like you, Dr. Francesca Cunningham."

"Your grand-aunt proposed marriage on your behalf five minutes ago," she told him dryly. "But I turned you down. She wanted to breed the bad streak out of the family and she thought that my blood would be the correct antidote for it."

"You must have made an impression then. But you turned me down . . . sight unseen too. Wasn't that rather a shame?"

She stuck her hands in her pockets and smiled up at him.

"It may be a libel. I doubt it is, for really you're a most attractive young man. You may not be aware of it, but you've got quite a reputation in the village . . . for breaking hearts. They tell me that you break every available female heart for a radius of five miles, as the crow flies . . . round Harton Parish Church.''

"And you believed them?'' he asked reproachfully.

"Now I've met you, I believe them all the more.''

"Are all women doctors like you?'' he asked her and she shook her head and got into the car, screwing down the window to look out at him.

"I hope not.''

He looked at her quizzically.

"So Esmond is the lucky man?''

"And why is Ess-mond a lucky man?''

"Because you'll marry him of course.''

She shook her head at him scornfully and then smiled.

"My poor young friend! You couldn't be further off target. I'm as likely to marry Simon, the cat . . . and good day to you!''

When Francesca got back to Regent House at lunch time, she rang the hospital again and was heartened to find that Rachael Monk's condition had improved. She went upstairs to tell Esmond the news and to discuss the visits with him and found that Connie had just brought him lunch up on a tray and was pouring out chicken soup from a silver bowl.

"That's all he'll eat for me today, no matter how I tempt him. It's not enough to keep a mouse alive, yet alone a grown man."

She went off and was back in two minutes with a second tray for Francesca, and a saucer of chopped liver for Simon.

"I've brought you your omelet and you can have it here. It will keep Dr. Ross company and cheer him up, for he's fretting to be back at work and maybe you can persuade him to have some sense and stay where he is."

She paused at the door on her way downstairs.

"You can tell him how you got on at the Grange. He's been worrying himself about it all the morning."

Francesca could never resist an opportunity to play one of her games with Connie, Esmond thought, as he saw a confidential look creep over his assistant's face, saw the sideways glance of her eyes, in his direction.

"Miss Mallory and I got on like a house on fire. She even asked me to marry Lucien."

Connie turned back into the room, her eyes popping wide open.

"I don't believe a word of that. You're only saying it to annoy Dr. Esmond."

"And why should that annoy you, Essmond?"

"It appears to annoy Connie too," Esmond said. "And really, it's a pretty incredible statement."

She looked demure and prim, but he could see that she was bubbling over with mischief.

"It's true. On my word of honour! Miss Mallory was quite keen on the idea . . . something to do with genetics. She wanted my blood to water down some bad blood the Mallorys are supposed to have. I turned the proposition down, there and then."

"Well that's a relief anyway," put in Connie sarcastically, more amused with the conversation than Esmond. He had picked up his spoon and was looking at the soup in distaste.

"Did you meet the young man?" she asked, and Francesca put back her head and laughed.

"Indeed I met him . . . in the most dramatic circumstances too. I ran him down on his own drive. I came round that last corner too

fast and he was right in my path. He was very
put out about it, till he saw it wasn't you, Ess-
mond. Then he calmed down a bit. He's very
attractive you know. I don't know if I
shouldn't have taken the old lady's suggestion
more seriously. . . ."

She shot a glance at the housekeeper's face
and was delighted at the interested expression
she saw there. She never failed to enjoy taking a rise out of Connie.

"I told him all about it and he was tickled
pink. If I'd played my cards right, I'm convinced that I could have got him to ratify the
proposal there and then. He said I was
fabulous, Mistress Constance . . . said I'd got
fire. What do you think of that for a first
impression?"

"I hope you don't get burnt with your
fabulous fire. That's what I think. You
should be ashamed of yourself."

She bustled out of the room, pretending to
be very indignant and Esmond thought how
childish and silly were these constant battles
of wit. He had put down his spoon, like a
sulky schoolboy and he turned his face
sideways on the pillow.

"I suppose I should warn you about
Mallory," he began slowly, in a serious way

that did not match the levity of the conversation in the least. "I think I told you he had a bad reputation, but——"

She looked at him quickly and saw that in some way, he had been hurt by the conversation. It was almost as if he were jealous of her interest in Lucien Mallory, but that was so fantastic an idea that she put it out of her head. He had obviously thought that she had meant what she said . . . that Lucien attracted her. She set her omelet down in front of the fire and came to sit on the bed.

"You needn't warn me. Perhaps it's time I told you a story . . . a sad and secret story, but you must drink your soup as I go along."

He smiled at her and took a spoonful of soup to oblige her.

"It happened a long time ago," she began, as if she told a child a story, and he realised that she was going to confide in him. For some reason, she was going to tell him about her love affair . . . about the vaccination against love. The mirth had died in her eyes and she was in deadly earnest for all the way her lips smiled still.

"I was young at the time and not particularly talented or beautiful, but I had what Charles Dickens called a loving heart, or

Murdo said I had. I gave this same loving heart to a young man and I was happy for a while. The happiness lasted till I found out that he was polygamous. That was his word . . . not mine. He told me quite calmly that all men were polygamous and that I must learn to put up with it. . . ."

A north-east wind blew in her voice . . . shrill and biting and cruel and her eyes were desolate.

"I found him in damning circumstances with a married woman. She was a greater fool than I was, but that was no consolation at the time. 'It was just one of those things,' he told me. He still loved me and would love me till he died, but I must be sophisticated. I must grow up. I must realise, once and for all, the different nature of men. As they say in the Bible, I went out from his presence, a leper as white as snow. . . . If I had been burning over a slow fire, the agony in my breast couldn't have been worse. Only for Murdo, I'd have died. He had warned me about Paulus. That was the man's name. At least, it was Paul, but I called him Paulus . . . thought it romantic. I suppose that was the erudition of St. Catherine's."

She made a grimace of self-deprecation and

picked up his soup plate, now empty, though he had not noticed as he drank it. She fetched the omelet, by right hers, from in front of the fire and put it on his tray, put the fork in his hand and he ate it like a mechanical man, so engrossed was he in her story. . . . Then she picked Simon up and cradled him in her arms, as if to draw comfort from his soft body.

"Murdo had warned, just as you were going to do a moment ago. You have the same kindness as Murdo has. I'm telling you all this, just to show you . . . to prove to you, that it isn't necessary. I didn't listen to Murdo. I knew it all. I was full of youthful self-confidence. It's funny how one thinks that one will be the one woman to hold the gay charmer. Even if he's like King Hal, you say, 'I'm not going to be one of the divorced . . . beheaded . . . died. . . .' "

"So you went to Murdo?" he put in gently, for she was silent for a space, and she got up abruptly and went to stand at the window with her back to him. He thought there were tears in her voice when she spoke again, her chin against the cat's head.

"I went to Murdo, like the child I was, burnt by the fire I'd been told to leave alone.

I wanted to be dead . . . like Rachael today, I wanted to find the nothingness of death . . . to escape into it to hide from my pain, especially when he was so gentle and kind . . . this old Murdo, whom I would have seen dead for my handsome brave Paulus. . . ."

One hand went out to grip the sill of the window and she had hardened her voice to sarcasm at the thought of her younger self, yet there was sadness in it, that she could not hide, and regret, and still, that hint of tears.

"Paulus went off and got himself another girl . . . and another. He has a practice in Birmingham now and a wife and three children, and it's all done with and forgotten, except that technically, I'm without a heart. It was impossible to replace it. For all Murdo's kindness, I didn't want to have a heart again. I had no use for it. I would never willingly face the pain of losing it all over again. You understand all this fanciful talk of mine?"

"It's not fanciful. It's good of you to give me your confidence, but you're making yourself unhappy. . . ."

She spun round to smile at him.

"Oh, no, I'm not unhappy. I don't miss my

heart the least little bit. I'm armoured against unhappiness."

"And that's the end of the story?" he asked her and wanted to take her into his arms and kiss the unhappiness from her eyes, but she was shaking her head.

"That's a closed chapter, but today I met another man for the first time . . . a man as like Paulus as his twin brother, the fair hair falling, just so, over his forehead, his eyes sparkling with fun."

"So?" he prompted her. "It's Lucien Mallory then? You weren't joking when you said you found him attractive?"

"I thought today what a comfortable thing it is to have no heart . . . to have gained wisdom . . . to remember the pain of heroic surgery without an anaesthetic . . . to have been burnt by the fire and know to avoid it . . . to know it can't happen again."

She came across to sit on the bed by his side and spilled Simon out of her arms, her gaiety back, switched on suddenly, as if the sun had come out to brighten the room.

"You must be bored to death with all this nonsense. I thought it best to tell you. There's no need to warn me about Lucien or about anybody else. I can't fall in love . . . I've learnt my lesson well. . . ."

Connie had come into the room and was studying the empty plate with satisfaction.

"Did he finish his soup, Dr. Frankie?"

There was a golden web of happiness all about her again, that entangled the whole room in its meshes.

"And my omelet, Connie . . . every last bit."

He was all embarrassment suddenly.

"Good Lord! Was that omelet yours? I'm most infernally sorry. Haven't you had any lunch? I don't know how I could have done such a thing. I wasn't even hungry."

"It was a lucky thing for Simon that he ate up his liver so quickly today, Connie. I don't like to think what might have happened."

She crossed to the door and stood looking back.

"I'm going downstairs to make myself a sandwich. Perhaps we should move those cowslips from the bedside table to the mantelpiece?"

When they had gone, he lay back against the pillows and tried to figure out why Francesca had told him her story. Perhaps it had only been to show him that she could not be hurt by Mallory, but it seemed to go farther than that. It seemed that she was warning him not to fall in love with her himself. It was far too late for such a warning . . . far too late to turn off the emotion, that overwhelmed him, so that she was never out of his thoughts any moment of the day . . . so that she inhabited all his dreams too. Surely it was not hopeless? Surely, given much cherishing, she could be healed of the hurt that life had dealt her at an early and impressionable age. She was so lovely. She had bewitched him and filled his life with life and light and happiness. He thought of the dimples, that winked at the sides of her small pointed chin and put out a hand to stroke the cat, that lay by his side.

"When you purr at my lady like that, Simon, I'm well aware of what you're telling her . . . and I think she is too. '*Vicisti*, thou hast conquered'."

It was a week later, when Inspector Taylor and Sergeant Bullen called to see Dr. Ross. Connie showed them up to the bedroom, where Esmond was still an unwilling prisoner, and Simon stood up, as they came into the room, stretched himself and yawned, then he graciously accepted Bullen's greetings and allowed himself to be tickled behind the ears. Taylor had extracted a bundle of letters from his jacket pocket and was snapping off the elastic band.

"We were right about there being some more of these about, sir. That's the total bag to date. Even the sarge here has got one, with a nice set of prints too. We'd be glad of your views. You must be familiar with the local 'possibles'."

He handed the letter to Esmond and Bullen grinned.

"Mine is highly libellous, sir. I'm glad Dr. Cunningham isn't here all the same. She'd say 'I believe you, Master Bullen. Thousands wouldn't.' "

They had not noticed that she had come into the room till she spoke.

"And why should I say that?"

She stood by the bedside and put out a finger to touch the top letter.

"I saw the police car outside. I thought I'd come in to hear the news. Any fresh developments?"

Taylor's voice was as clipped and precise as ever, as he itemised the facts for them.

"The gum used is the same brand as that

sold in the Harton Post Office Stores . . . notepaper too and envelopes. Bullen's letter had a faint scent of lavender . . . not obtained in his pocket, he tells me. The writing is done by an aquamarine ball point pen, cost eight-pence, also freely obtainable in the Stores. The dust-men couldn't help us . . . nothing out of the ordinary there, but we've got a lovely set of prints, so it's only a matter of time before we have the criminal."

She sat down suddenly as if her legs would not support her. After a terrified glance at their faces, she buried her own face in her hands and her shoulders shook with sobs.

"Inspector," she said in a muffled voice. "Sergeant Bullen. Oh, Sergeant, you were suspicious of me from that first day. You knew. . . . What can I say? It's no use going on, is it . . . day after day, with justice closing in on me? If you knew the strain it's been . . . and the relief to confess it all. I don't know what got into me . . . some innate evil in my heart . . . some awful dark frustration because women get the dirty end of the stick. They say it's always the woman pays. I don't know, but I confess . . . I confess openly. . . ."

She looked up and saw Esmond's face staring at her in horror. Then she took a pen from her pocket and inked the tips of her fingers one by one. She sighed as she picked up one of the envelopes and executed a set of prints on it with great concentration. Then she offered it to Bullen with downcast head.

"Here's your evidence, Master Bullen. I'll come quietly. Don't handcuff me before the neighbours. You know how people talk in Harton. . . ."

Taylor and the sergeant were laughing at her ridiculous performance, but Esmond was feeling a strong desire to lay her across his knee and give her a taste of what she called Murdo's justice. Then he smiled at the thought of the surprise it might cause the two policemen, if he gave way to his inclination.

"Really Francesca! Your childish sense of humour'll get you into trouble one of these days."

"I'm sorry."

She slid to her knees by the bedside and for a moment, he thought it was her way of apologising to make him smile at her. Then she took his hand and inked his fingers one by one. She leaned over to take the envelope back from Bullen and executed his prints carefully and neatly beneath her own. She went off to the bathroom then and fetched a sponge and a clean linen towel and she cleaned the ink off their fingers, leaving a good proportion of it on the towel.

"I don't know what Connie will say when she sees that towel," Taylor remarked. "You're in real trouble there, lady."

"We'll not meet catastrophe till we come face to face with it," she smiled and threw it under the bed out of sight. Then she curled herself up, like a cat herself beside Simon, at Esmond's feet and stretched out a hand to pick Bullen's letter up.

"Let's see what the sergeant has been up to. . . ."

Inspector Taylor was thinking that she drifted round the room in a very familiar way and he wondered if they were lovers. Then he thought of Ross's face, when his lady had taken his hand in hers to ink his fingers and knew that they were not any such thing. She had no self-consciousness, but perhaps lady doctors were like that . . . used to seeing men in bed. The relationship was a bedside manner on her part, whatever it was on his . . . and she was teasing old Bullen out of his life, just because Bullen had thought she might be guilty and she had caught him at it, or so Bullen said. She was going to make the most

211

of pulling his leg about the letter. Her mouth was quirking upwards at the sides, as she read it.

"Dear Sergeant,
 I do not know if you're aware of the behaviour of one of the constables in Harton, but they're all at the same game and they're a rotten streak in the English Police Force. . . ."

The words leapt out at Francesca and all her gaiety was gone in a flash. . . .

A rotten streak in the English Police Force. . . .

She closed her eyes for a moment and was back in the bedroom at the Grange with the faint scent of lavender in her nostrils. She had said "I'm going to marry no one" or words to that effect and the old lady had said that if she married Lucien, she might breed the rotten streak out of the Mallory family. It was impossible. Yet was it? The first Lucien's wife had gone to an asylum near Bedford and insanity was a thing that sometimes cropped up down the generations. She picked up the letters and leafed through them quickly and in the last one, she had it again.

"Dear Vicar,

It's well known that you keep these *au pair* girls for your own purposes. Your wife's heart is broken and if justice were done, those girls of yours would be whipped. . . ."

"You deserve a whipping for blasphemy." That's what Charlotte Mallory had said to her.

She uncurled herself from the bed and walked over to the window to look out at the cottages on the other side of the road, her hands clasped tightly behind her back.

"I know your criminal, Inspector Taylor," she said in a small voice and he leaped to his feet as though she had given him an electric shock. Then he grinned and sat down again.

"It's another of your jokes," he laughed. "You caught me again that time, lady."

She did not turn round, only shook her head slightly and he went over to stand behind her, his voice incredulous.

"You mean that you actually know who wrote those letters Dr. Cunningham? Oh, come now, this isn't a game, you know."

"I've no proof . . . at least nothing that would stand up in court. I'd rather not make accusations. . . ."

He was on to her now, like a terrier after a rat, all policeman in a flash, as he wheeled round to pick up the letters and leaf through them.

"It's something you've spotted in these letters? It must be."

"It's a matter of professional secrecy. I can't tell you who it is. I think I can stop the letters. Will that content you?"

"Of course it won't. It's your duty to divulge what you know. Medical etiquette doesn't come into it."

"You think it's one of our patients . . . a woman, you've attended?" Esmond demanded and she still kept her eyes fixed on the burnt umber of the cottage thatch.

"So you think it's a woman?" she murmured and Bullen's voice was rough, as he declared that of course it was a woman. Then he thought how forlorn she looked with them all against her.

"I believe you, Sergeant . . . thousands wouldn't. Please to stop the inspector bullying me."

She turned back into the room and went to stand by the fire, her hands gripping the mantelshelf, as she watched the flames flickering up the chimney.

"It is a patient . . . or I think it is. Have you noticed that I'm no longer the target? She's sick in mind . . . sicker than any of us thought, but she's past hurting anybody physically. It wouldn't help to release the full force of the law on her. The letters are only a symptom of her disease . . . might never have been sent in happier circumstances. I'll deal with it myself."

"You will in no circumstances deal with it yourself," Esmond told her abruptly. "You'll tell us the name of this person at once and stop all this foolish nonsense of yours."

She turned to face him at last.

"I'm sorry, Ess-mond. It's something I've got to do . . . try to do. I hope that I'll be able to tell you, one of these days, that there'll be no more letters . . . and that will be the end of it. Oh, damn what life can do to people! I'm sorry, will you excuse me?"

She was through the door in an instant, before anybody could stop her . . . a Francesca as different from her usual self, as to make it seem impossible. She stayed away from Regent House, till she had to return at dinner time and she refused to discuss the matter with Esmond, although he had a stormy scene with her. Over the next day or two, there was a coolness between them and he was silent and distant. She was very glad when Pat came home for the holidays and the tension eased. Esmond had no way of knowing that she had visited the Grange on the morning after the police had called. She had stood at the foot of Miss Mallory's bed, knowing that she was far too inexperienced to deal with the problem. She had sent Ellen Ferguson away and she looked at the old lady and wondered if her suspicions could possibly be true.

"I've come to see you about something unpleasant. What I'm going to say may cause you pain. . . ."

The white hair shone in the light as the old lady bent her head graciously and again, the diamond rings winked and sparkled.

"I'm sure you're not a person to cause unnecessary pain, Dr. Francesca."

"People have been receiving anonymous letters in the village . . . I got one myself and I've seen others. The police have been called in, for they must be stopped."

"Indeed, I agree. If I can help you in any way. . . ."

She was not the slightest bit put out and Francesca wondered if she could have been

216

wrong after all. Anybody could have used those phrases . . . a person in close contact with Miss Mallory. It would be the easiest thing in the world for Ellen Ferguson to have picked up that turn of speech. She felt her way along and was more unsure of herself than ever.

"The letters are coming from this house . . . I know who's responsible for them. I know they are a symptom of mental illness. . . ."

The arthritic hand had crept out to pleat the sheet into tiny folds and the old eyes had dropped from hers.

"It's a thing, that might happen to any of us . . . might even happen to a lady like yourself, Miss Mallory, and I'm sorry for the person, nothing else. I'm willing to help too, if you'd like to talk to me about it, for we'll have to fix the matter up between us . . . you and I."

"You know who wrote them?" Miss Mallory asked in a breathless little voice. "Oh, dear! What are you going to do? The police . . .?"

"If I tell the police, they'll come here and search and they'll find the evidence they're looking for. There'll be a deal of trouble and disgrace and it's not necessary. Just give me your promise that there'll be no more of these foolish letters and the matter will rest there. That's all I want . . . your word as a lady. . . ."

The old eyes were shrewd, as they met hers for an instant and then dropped again to watch the hand, that went on pleating the sheet.

"I give you my word. You're a kind gel to let me know what was going on in my own house. It's my duty to clean my own midden out and I'll see to it . . . and now, if you'd excuse me. I don't feel well. Send Ellen up to me, please, as you go out."

She had felt more uncertain of herself than ever, as she went down the stairs. The interview had been so brief and vague. She regretted that she had not confided in Esmond. After all, Miss Mallory was his patient and he would have dealt more competently with the whole thing . . . probably would have kept the police out of it. If the letters still went on and she had to tell him eventually . . . tell the police too, of her feeble attempts this morning, she would be in big trouble.

She kept away from the upstairs bedrooom in Regent House as much as she could, and she went about her work doggedly with the worry never far from her mind that she had made a mess of the whole case. Then Don Jones came out and allowed Esmond downstairs and the time came, when she went into Wentbridge Station to meet Pat's train. It seemed to her that Pat broke all the tension into smithereens, as she ran across the sitting-room, in her navy-blue overcoat and school hat and threw herself into her father's arms. He unwound the red and white knitted scarf and helped Pat off with her hat and coat, drew her to sit on a cushion at his feet.

"You don't know how good it is to have you home, Patricia. They've been bullying me to death . . . Connie and Francesca too. At least, I'll have an ally now."

He looked at Francesca and the friendliness was back in his eyes. Whatever black mood he had been in, had vanished. There was a change in his attitude to his daughter too. Connie was delighted with it and wondered what magic the lady doctor had done to get him to regard Pat as a human being at last. She had certainly planned a mild round of social entertainments for them, but there seemed nothing more definite. Perhaps her very presence had altered him in some way, had made him behave like any loving father. He seemed delighted to take them to the

cinema and the theatre. Once they drove out
to the east coast for a picnic. The four weeks
of the holiday ran away very happily and the
poison pen letters were almost forgotten and
then a formal invitation arrived for them to
dine at the Grange with Miss Mallory.

Francesca dressed with care for her first
appearance in Harton society with her
principal. She put on a dark green velvet
dress and appeared at Regent House half an
hour before they were due to leave. Pat was
still upstairs and she was glad, for once, to
have got the opportunity to speak to Esmond
by himself, for a report had come from the
hospital about Rachael Monk and she wanted
his advice. His eyes appraised her, as she
came into the sitting-room and he stood up to
greet her.

"I've had the letter from Ozzie Caston
Price, Ess-mond. It came on this afternoon's
post and Nurse brought it round to me."

He knew by her face that it was bad news.
She looked unusually troubled as she held the
letter out to him and he put on his horn-
rimmed glasses and looked down at it.

"Dear Frankie,
    As you say, this poor child's problems seem

never ending. I note that she was discharged from hospital after her attempted suicide and that her pregnancy carried on normally, till you had some doubts about the infant's head on her last ante-natal visit to you. I agree with your findings and am referring her for X-ray. I will append the report at the end of this letter.

How are you enjoying general practice? Have you quite forgotten that rosy dream of specialisation that we both had when you were my registrar?"

In Caston Price's own hand under his signature, came the postscript. . . .

"X-rays confirm the presence of an anencephalus of thirty-six weeks maturity. It would seem advisable to admit her for induction at once. There seems no point in prolonging such a pregnancy. I have not told either her or her rather peculiar parents."

Esmond returned the letter and went to pour her a glass of sherry.

"I went up to see Monk this afternoon . . . told him about the child's deformity. I wanted to arrange to send Rachael in at once. They

221

had a bed, but Monk turned the idea down flat . . . won't hear of interfering with nature, as he put it."

He came across to put the glass of sherry into her hand.

"You made it clear to him that the child can't survive?" he asked her. "Of course, it might live for a moment or two but that's all."

She went to stand at the mantelpiece, sipping her sherry and her face was worried and sad, as she told him that she had argued back and forth with Monk for an hour or more.

"I gave him a full picture, Ess-mond. Told him brutally at last that there'd be no top to its head, but he asked me if the child had a better chance of being born alive, if we didn't interfere. I had to say yes. He insists that it be given the chance of breathing and so to be issued with its immortal soul."

"So?" he asked, thinking how green her eyes were against the soft velvet of the dress.

"Surely God isn't so meticulous about whether one of his creatures takes a breath or not? Monk holds that a still-born child has no soul. It has been moving and living inside its mother's body. Are the rules so rigorous that

222

one moment one way or the other makes all that difference? Even Monk's God of the Old Testament can't be such a bloody fool, can He?"

He smiled at her outburst and reminded her that such language didn't match up with her pretty dress.

"Don't try to side-track me, Ess-mond. It can't all be so hide-bound and cut and dried and stupid . . . and cruel."

"Monk's rules are laid down for him in black and white in his family Bible. By the way, is he your sender of the poison pen letters. Did you say 'she' to put us off the track?"

"I won't be put off the subject. Don't keep switching the topic of conversation. Tell me if you believe that a stillborn child is deprived of all hope of heaven, just because it hasn't managed to get outside its mother's body and breathe?"

She was at her most attractive with her brows drawn down like that, he thought irrelevantly, wondering what she would do, if he went across the room and took the glass out of her hand, put it on the mantelpiece . . . if he took her into his arms and kissed her. He felt inclined to risk it.

"Do you?" she reiterated.

"Monk's rules may be different from mine."

"He thinks that God has laid a hand upon him to punish him, like it says in the scriptures, 'God chastiseth those He loveth' . . . or some such thing."

He laughed at that and said it sounded like Murdo's judgement. It was time to shift her from her serious mood.

"You can't help admiring the way he's stuck by his code all the same," he remarked. "He's going to see to it that Rachael has her baby, when the Lord thinks fit and not Caston Price or your good self. He's leaving the issue in God's hands, isn't he?"

"And he's decided that the baby's to be born at home," she grumbled. "Think of it, Ess-mond, in that cottage. He's blaming Rachael for the fact the baby's deformed. She's sinned in attempting to take her own life. Now she's to be punished for it. We had a frightful bust-up this afternoon. He told me that she had called down the wrath of Jehovah on her unborn infant . . . and I told him that he was an ignorant, bigoted, superstitious old fool and that I'd have him locked up, if it was within my power."

224

"And what did he say to that?"

"He as near as damn it, gave me a taste of Murdo's judgement. I had called down the wrath of Zachary Monk on my head, or so it seemed."

He took the glass from her hand at last and smiled at her earnest face.

"We'll call down Miss Mallory's wrath on our heads, if we don't get along to the Grange. What on earth's keeping Patricia? She should have been ready ages ago, but she was lying in a hot bath and her bath essence makes the whole infernal house stink like a French brothel."

It was no good letting the miseries of the practice darken one's whole existence. One must detach one's thoughts from the problems of life and push the sadness into the back of one's mind. She looked sideways at him and smiled.

"And you have experience of such an establishment, Monsieur?" she demanded, and he protested that her humour was still tinged with the hospital staff-room.

"I'm going to make a formal complaint about it, when next we go to Oxford to see your guardian. I never know what you're going to say next. Don't come out with any of that stuff at the Grange, or—I'll be asked to take you home. . . ."

She remembered the letters that Miss Mallory's hand had presumably contrived and wondered if crude humour was as foreign to Miss Mallory, as Esmond imagined it to be. He sat opposite her in the big dining-room an hour later and watched his lady assistant strike sparks off Lucien Mallory. The young man was setting his cap at her, he thought irritably. He had kissed her hand in a ridiculous way, when they arrived and they had talked nonsense about the old lady's pro-posal of marriage on his behalf, as if it was the most tremendous joke.

"I won't go back on Aunt's word," Lucien had laughed. "She tells me you're worried about my reputation, but I'll turn over a new leaf. I'll never look at any other woman as long as I live. Who would, if they were married to you?"

She had not been in the least put out by it. She had wrinkled her nose at him and Miss Mallory had sat in her wheel chair, cackling like a witch.

"A leopard can't change his spots, Miss Mallory. Besides, it would be the devil to keep staff."

"She's well able for you, Lucy. What do you say to that?"

One of the Goodge girls had come into the room then and she had giggled. It would be all over the village in the morning.

"I'd attract a supply of pretty girls into the house," Mallory had laughed. "It'd be an advantage. What girl would take a job at the Vicarage, when she thought of my charms here?"

"Hm!" she had frowned. "One moment ago, you weren't going to look at another woman."

Even Pat was enjoying it, laughing all over her face and showing the erudition of St. Catherine's by crying out "*Quod erat demonstrandum!*"

"She has you there, Lucy," the old woman had chuckled. "You'll not find another like her. You're a fool if you don't run off to Gretna with her this minute."

Esmond had been irritated beyond measure at the conversation. He had frowned at the ridiculous spectacle of Mallory taking the girl through the double doors to the hall, whispering in her ear, but loudly in a stage whisper, to make sure they all heard it.

"The Vanden Plas is at the door, my lady.

Dr. Ross won't mind if we borrow it. What do you say to my Aunt's latest proposition?"

It had gone on like that the entire evening and Ross had sulked like a young man in his teens . . . and been surprised at his own feelings. He had taken Francesca back to Nurse Roberts's house finally and had said good night to her very curtly. On the way home, Patricia put her arms round his neck from the back seat.

"Frankie's marvellous, Daddy, She's such fun. It's wonderful to have somebody in the house to talk to."

"You've had Connie," he pointed out sharply, and felt her breath against his cheek in a deep sigh.

"Connie's different. She's grand, of course, but Frankie . . . you can talk to her about any single thing and not be ashamed of it. You've got no idea of the things she's helped me with. I was getting a crush on Lucien and she told me he was a flirt and not to get involved. If you don't leave that sort of thing too late, she said, you can laugh yourself out of it. That's what we were doing tonight and I'm not hurt any more. She never thinks things are silly. She sorts out all my problems for me and explains how emotions work. . . ."

Again, he felt the soft breath against his cheek and pitied the defencelessness of her.

"Do you like her, Daddy?"

"Indeed I do."

"She was only joking with Lucien tonight. It was a campaign we had planned. You didn't know that and you were put out because you thought it wasn't dignified enough for the practice. It was only fun. She doesn't like Lucian one little bit, but she admires you terribly. She looks at you a lot, when she thinks you're not looking at her."

He was amazed at the pleasure the words gave him.

"It would be a good thing, if she got to love you, wouldn't it?" she asked him softly, ruffling the hair at the back of his neck with a finger. "Then you could get married . . . that is, if you got to love her too. It's always been marvellous to come home, of course, but now it's special. It's like a little enchanted land of happiness . . . sparkling . . . shining . . . fun. . . ."

Indeed it was a very apt description, he thought, as he turned the car into the front drive and leaned over to open the door for her.

"Could you get to . . . like her a lot? She's really very nice, you know."

"I like her a lot now," he laughed. Then he took her through the door into the hall, with an arm round her shoulders, hugged close to his side, as he had not done since she was six years old.

Francesca had a conversation with Sergeant Bullen on somewhat the same subject the next morning, when she came out of a patient's house on rounds and found him waiting for her at the door of her car. They exchanged greetings and then he came to the pitch of the matter he had in mind.

"I suppose you wouldn't like to tell me all about it off the record, Dr. Cunningham? Those letters seem to have stopped."

"You suppose right," she smiled, as he opened the car door for her.

"And you did manage to fix it up without our help then? And there'll be no more of the filthy things?"

She shook her head at him as she got into the car and screwed down the window to talk to him.

"I'm not at that stage yet. I'll come to it eventually, I hope. I'll tell you exactly what

I've done. I've bunged up the hole in the dyke with a cork and I've got my fingers crossed that it'll hold. It's just as likely to fly out and hit me between the two eyes. Then I'll find myself up that creek of yours without a paddle and the waters rising fast . . . and if that does happen, you'll please to be on my side and not range yourself with the big guns, that will be trained against me . . . like you did on another regrettable occasion."

"You wouldn't say that before Dr. Ross . . . not that bit about the creek," he challenged her.

"So I'm afraid of Dr. Ross now?" she grimaced. "Well, perhaps I am at that. He's very superior and grave and serious. I suppose that I'm impulsive and temperamental and liable to go off at half cock, but I assure you that I find him a steadying influence all the same. I'm improving, don't you think?"

"That's not what they're saying this morning in the village, Doctor."

She looked at him in pretended dismay.

"What's to do now?"

"They say there was a very grand dinner party last night and that a certain young lady looked irresistible in a green velvet dress with a low cut bodice. They say that the Lord of the Manor is head over heels in love with her and can talk of nobody but the fabulous Francesca Cunningham."

"The Harton grapevine is way off today, Master Bullen," she smiled and he put both his hands on the car roof and leaned down to speak more confidentially.

"They say that the doctor is taking it hard. He was as black as a thunder-cloud the whole evening. He didn't eat any of his dinner, even though it was roast pheasant, which is his favourite. They say that he almost punched Mr. Lucien's head, when that young gent had the cheek to kiss the lady's hand. . . ."

"They say . . . they say . . . they say . . ." she laughed. "Really, I'm surprised at you to listen to such tittle-tattle and there's not a word of truth in the whole account."

His eyes were serious suddenly and she looked up at him in surprise, for she had thought it an amusing game. She had found that the sergeant had the same propensity for nosing out amusing situations as Connie had.

"I wouldn't like you to make a mistake about an important thing . . . marriage for example. So don't be, what was it, impulsive and temperamental and liable to go off at half cock just now."

She gripped the steering wheel till her hands ached and looked ahead of her up the road, wondering what on earth he was getting at.

"Marriage, Master Bullen? I once told a gentleman that I'm not available as a wife."

"He proposed then?" he asked abruptly. "The doctor proposed and you turned him down?"

She turned to smile at him, but he detected a poignancy in her expression.

"He was eight years old or thereabouts . . . this gentleman, and he didn't offer for my hand. I told him that I had dedicated myself to the Royal Canadian Mounted Police, when I was his age . . . and that later on I gave my life to the healing of the sick . . . and am immune to men."

"That seems a bit of a shame, miss. The men may not be immune to you, but about those two other gentlemen we discussed . . . one is worth three hundred thousand of the other. I've known them both a long time . . . and I like you, ever since the day I was so foolish to think you might have been guilty of writing those letters . . . and you read my mind . . . and let me off so lightly . . . so if the immunity was to wear thin. . . ."

She cut in on him sharply.

"This very worthy gentleman of yours, I think you're way off the mark, Sergeant. He's not aware of the lady except as a playful and amusing kitten and after all, why should she object? She has those qualities."

"Does she object, doctor?"

"I'd take it kindly if you'd stop cross-examining me. You're getting as bad as Inspector Taylor."

Her next discussion on the subject was in Oxford. She dropped Pat off at St. Catherine's and went on to visit Murdo for the day at the end of the holidays and as usual, she gave him her confidence. She told him all about the dinner party and Lucien Mallory and what Sergeant Bullen had said. The whole story seemed to spill out suddenly and it came to an end, as she sipped her after dinner coffee rather miserably.

"This laddie back in college, you know who I mean. He's all over and done with, but could we take him out of the cupboard for a wee while?"

She nodded her head and went to sit against

his knee in her favourite position on the floor.

"He's mixed up with this some way, isn't he, Frankie?"

"Lucien Mallory is very like him to look at. That's all. No, it's not all. He's as like him as two peas in a pod . . . mentally and physically too."

"History is to repeat itself then? You're in love with this Mallory fellow and he's another of the polygamous kind, and you're full of fear at the future?"

She shook her head but said nothing and he pursued her with "Truly?"

"Truly."

"So you're in love with King Cophetua himself?"

His voice was so full of delight that she looked at him in surprise and then shook her head again, and again he challenged her.

"Truly?"

She leaned her head against his knee, not far from tears.

"I'm not going to fall in love again, Murdo. I'm too much of a coward. Anyhow I'd be no good for His Majesty, who still loves his dead queen. He thinks that I'm a shallow, amusing frivolous child and indeed I behave like one too. That's all there is to it."

He gripped her shoulder and swung her to face him.

"He's not in love with his dead queen. He never was in love with her. It was an infatuation he got at an early, impressionable age, but more about it I will not tell you and don't expect it of me. He's never known what it is to be in love with a lovely, accomplished, desirable, attractive, humorous, sincere, charming woman, till the last few weeks."

"I didn't know he knew somebody like that. . . ."

He looked down at her and shook his head.

"I hold the mirror up to you, my bonnie bairn . . . and you can't recognise your own self in it."

"Oh, Murdo, that's nonsense. You mean I'm humorous and lovely and all that? Merciful heavens! You think that Ess-mond is in love with me? Oh, no! You couldn't be further wrong."

"I'm not wrong. I'm always right. Just you quote me one instance when I haven't been right about you," he challenged her and she bent her head to study the carpet, under her feet and the colour crept up into her cheeks.

"He called me 'Kit' the other day. He let it slip by accident and he could have bitten his tongue out afterwards. It was some secret name he had for me. He admitted it . . . made a joke of it and said it was short for 'Kitten quality,' because he thought it suited me . . . not quite as adult as Simon, or so he said."

He tousled her hair about her face and laughed at her.

"A man doesn't have secret names for a lassie for nothing," he teased her.

He could not convince her that he was right. They talked on for hours and the time slipped away. It was far too late, before she started for home.

"At any rate, I've laid a ghost," he said at the last moment. "Two ghosts if I speak truly, for Lucien Mallory doesn't come into it . . . and neither does Sheelagh Ross. She never has come into it. So it's between Esmond Alexander Ross and your own self. There's no haste about. Let things run on for a wee while. One day you'll come back to see me . . . put your two arms about my neck. You'll say 'Murdo, my old baboon, you were right, as you're always right, when all's said and done . . . my Second Gentleman!' "

"You'll never be anything but the First Gentleman. There's nobody ever going to take your place, now or ever. Don't say such an awfully sad thing, just when we're saying good-bye."

He stood on the edge of the pavement and smiled at her through the car window.

"It's in the natural order of things, my darling. It doesn't mean that you'll love me any the less, for that'll never happen. You'll just be he and he'll be you. You'll know that's the way it should be, when it comes about . . . and now away about your business. Take care of yourself . . . and haste ye back!"

It was an unpleasant night for the long drive home to Harton. There had been a high wind all the day, but as the night drew on, it had risen to gale force. After an hour, she drew in at a garage to get petrol and looked up at the trees, that tossed against the cloudy sky. There was a full moon, which gleamed palely down at her for a moment, before the dark, tumbling clouds engulfed it again.

"Nasty night to be out, miss," remarked the garage man at her side. "Hope you ain't got far to go."

"Wentbridge."

"I'd pull in at a hotel, if I wor you. There's a good one down the road a piece. There was trees coming down all over the country . . . had it on the late news. You don't want no

238

trees to come down across the top of your nice car. . . ."

She hardly noticed the storm, with the tempest of her own thoughts. The journey seemed to drag out into eternity and then suddenly she was coming into the outskirts of Harton. As she pulled up at the nurse's house, she was surprised to see that the clock on the dashboard stood at two. Of course, Nurse Roberts was in bed, but the light was still on in her room. She put the car into the garage and let herself into the hall, threw her coat and her head scarf on a chair and ran quickly up the stairs to tap softly on the nurse's door. Nurse Roberts was sitting up in bed, reading a book and she smiled reproachfully.

"I'm sorry, Robbie. I'm terribly late."

"You'd best go down to Regent House this minute and try to make your peace with Dr. Ross, for he's out of his mind about the lateness of the hour. You know you said you'd be back at nine o'clock and it's past two. He's been on the phone every half hour, for all that I promised him I'd ring him the minute you got back. He wanted to get in touch with the police and the hospital and everything else he could think of. The last time he rang, he was on for going out in the car to see if he'd meet you . . . thought you might have had a break-down."

"Oh dear! I'd better ring him at once."

"If I were you, I'd go down to the house. He'll not be so angry with you face to face, but I wouldn't like to think what he might say over the phone. He's had trees falling down on you and head-on smashes and I don't know what. When you turn up with nothing wrong, he's like to put you across his knee and spank you, like the mothers do, when their child runs across the road under a car and doesn't get hit."

As she ran down the stairs, the door bell rang. She opened the door and found Esmond on the step.

"Nurse Roberts . . ." he began. "I'm not going to delay any longer . . ."

He pulled himself up sharply, when he saw her.

"It's you, Kit. You're back at last. Oh, thank God! It's been such an awful night."

She walked before him into the sitting-room and switched on the light, turned to find that his relief had been replaced by anger.

240

"Where on earth have you been? Did you have an accident?"

"Murdo and I were talking. I didn't notice the time."

She kicked at the fire with her toe.

"It's almost out. I'll fetch some sticks. Then I'll make some coffee."

"Blast the fire . . . and blast making coffee!" he said roughly. "Do you know what hour of the night it is? Have you any conception of the worry you've caused us? I suppose it didn't enter your head to telephone and tell us, that you'd be late?"

She went out to the kitchen and brought back some kindling, knelt down before the fire and watched it catch alight.

"Roberts was worried sick about you."

"I've just been up to tell her I'm home. She's not been worried about me. You're the one, that's making the fuss about an hour or two."

"An hour or two!" he ejaculated. "It's five hours, Kit. There's a tempest raging outside, or hadn't you noticed?"

She smiled at him over her shoulder.

"There's one raging inside too, isn't there, Ess-mond?"

She had never seen him really angry before

and she felt a quiver of fear in her stomach.

"Don't be pert," he snapped at her. "It doesn't become you in the slightest, and besides, it's an infernal . . . infernal impertinence to a man of my age."

"I didn't mean to be impertinent, Essmond. It's true. I'd rather face the storm outside, than have to face you in here at this moment, but I wasn't being impertinent. Well, perhaps I was, but I only meant it as a joke."

"Of course you did. Everything's a joke to you . . . even the fact that other people are inconvenienced and worried because of your thoughtlessness."

"Don't be stuffy," she smiled. "I'm sorry. I've said I'm sorry, or have I? Did I forget?"

"You forgot to look after your luggage on your journey from Switzerland. You forgot to leave Oxford in time. You forgot to phone and let me know that you'd be late. You forgot to say you're sorry. Have you any excuse in the world for your disgraceful behaviour?"

She stood up and shook her head, wrinkling her nose up and making a rueful face at him to try to coax him into better humour with her.

"Only that I'll try to mend my ways in future."

He was not in the slightest way appeased.

"You're laughing at me now. Well, I see nothing humorous in the situation . . . and if you ever do such a thing again, I'll give you something, which will wipe that laugh off your face. I promise you."

He was in a fury with her. His face was white with anger, his eyes very dark. Yet this was the man who was in love with her, according to Murdo. She wished Murdo could see him now.

"I think you'd better go," she said, her face suddenly serious and as white as his own. "You'd better go, before you say something that we'll both regret."

At that, he spun on his heel and strode out of the room. The front door banged behind him and she heard the car drive off down the road. Then she went slowly across the room to lie on the couch. After a time, she turned over to bury her face in the pillow. She wept silently by herself there in the quiet room till she drifted into an uneasy sleep.

Two hours later, she was awakened by a loud knocking at the front door. She sat up with her heart pounding, not knowing who she was, nor where, nor what time of the day or the month or the year it was . . . in some nightmare void between waking and sleeping. Then she remembered Harton and the practice and the angry, white face of Esmond Alexander Ross, who, Murdo had said, loved her. She thought for a moment, that he had come back to the house, more angry than ever. She dismissed the idea as ludicrous, as the knocking came again, louder and more prolonged, and a frantic finger pressed the bell to an urgent shrilling ring, that vibrated through the whole house. It was Zachary Monk on the front step, his face livid in the light, streaming out from the hall.

"Please, can you come at once, miss? Rachael's had pains all the night and didn't say ought about them, till just now. She wakened her mother a while back . . . they wus so bad. It w'unt be long now. . . ."

She stood by the girl's bedside in a remarkably short time. As she put on her gown and mask and washed up at the old-fashioned wash-hand-stand, she had banished the thought of the scene with Esmond Ross out of her mind. She had known all along that Murdo had been talking nonsense. She tried to calm the emotional upheaval in her mind, but she felt very tired and in no way ready to face the drama, that would be enacted in Monk's cottage within the next hour. As she often did on such occasions, she spoke informally to God.

"Please don't turn your face away from what's to happen now. You said 'Suffer the little children . . .' I know this child can't live, but You know how important it is to Monk. Please let it breathe . . . be baptised . . . receive the cross on its forehead, Your cross. Surely they've suffered enough? Don't give them more than they can bear . . . and help me, as You never fail to help me. . . ."

She watched the steel tip of the stethoscope go down on Rachael's skin, as the nurse listened to the baby's heart. Her hair shone more brightly than the steel, and her face was very grave. In a little while, her whisper was at Francesca's ear.

"I can hardly get it now. It's rapid and uneven . . . fading to nothing. It won't last out another ten minutes of these sharp pains."

So all sufferings were going to be in vain, Francesca thought, as the gas-air machine snored with each deep breath. It would inevitably be a still birth . . . and if what

Zachary Monk believed was true, the child would be banished to some limbo . . . a void where such children lived for eternity away from the presence of God. Suppose that were true? The clock on the mantelpiece was sliding its hand round to five minutes, to ten, and still the pains flowed and ebbed like the tide. Then at last it had come into sight. Another five minutes, it would be born. Nurse Roberts was listening again for the infant's heart beat . . . nodding her head imperceptibly. Francesca put out a finger to touch the head. You couldn't baptise a child till it was born, and it wouldn't be born in time. She moved her hand to make the sign of the cross. You hadn't to say the words aloud. You thought them deep in your heart.

"I baptise thee in the name of the Father . . . and of the Son . . ."

Surely the Son would forgive her for her presumption, even if the God of Zachary Monk's Old Testament frowned down upon her. . . .

"And of the Holy Ghost. I baptise thee Mercy. I don't even know if the child is a boy or a girl, but mercy must be meted out to both impartially. Surely . . . surely . . ."

The nurse's face was telling her that the

child still lived, but in half a minute, she had taken the stethoscope from her ears and was straightening up, her lips forming the single word "Gone."

Well, she had performed the baptism, not according to the law of Caesar perhaps, but in the eyes of God, everything was possible. The time was sliding on and here was the infant now, dead as Nurse Roberts had predicted, gone indeed, but whither . . . a small girl like a malevolent frog, looking up at her out of dead eyes. Nurse Roberts whipped it up and away, wrapped it in a scrap of blanket and transferred it to the square cardboard box by the door. The room began to be frightening in its silence. The alarm clock ticked out the seconds still in a cheap tinny voice and that was all. Then an early car hummed by on the road outside and Rachael stirred and moaned a little, whimpered.

"Why ain't it crying? It's born, ain't it? Why is it all so quiet?"

It was time to drive in the thin edge of the wedge of fresh agony.

"It's a little girl, Rachael, but she's not well. We're doing what we can, but . . ."

Nurse Roberts was bending down to wipe the sweat from the pallid forehead.

"You've been very brave. Keep your eyes closed and take another breath from the mask. You're a very good girl. . . ."

The third stage was like lightning. Francesca left the nurse to finish tidying up and went wearily through to the kitchen at the back of the house, where Monk and his wife waited, their heads bowed, like statues of grief, one on either side of the black range.

"It was a girl . . . still-born. It didn't have a separate existence . . . it didn't live. . . ."

Monk's breath went out in a hiss of agony and Mrs. Monk buried her face in her apron. She leaned against the edge of the table and looked down at them, her breast wrung with pity.

"Maybe I got round those rules of yours. I believe so. The child wasn't born. I could only touch its head. It was still inside the womb . . . you understand. I baptised it, before it died. . . ."

She looked at the hope that was lighting up Monk's granite features . . . the face she had thought might belong to his his own harsh Jehovah. A doctor had the right . . . the honour to perform emergency baptism, but not before a baby had its own separate existence . . . not before it was a single, living, breathing entity.

"It'll have to be registered as a still birth. You understand? So legally, the child is unbaptised. Still, there are other courts . . . I called her Mercy."

Monk had grasped her hand in his and she was surprised to see the slow painful tears that formed in his eyes and overflowed down his cheeks.

"God bless you for what you done! I take back all the hard words I used against you. I'd like to see the child. I know you said not, and I promised you, but it ain't right not to see my own granddaughter, just because she ain't perfect."

There was no turning him from his purpose, but at least, she would not cause pain to Mrs. Monk. She sent her through to talk to Rachael and brought back the box, lifted the blanket. He uttered a cry of horror before he could check himself and recoiled a step or two with his hand to his face.

"It's a child o' Satan . . . it's the wages of sin. That ain't no child of Jehovah's."

She was almost too tired to think of the words to say to him, but she knew well that what she said in the next few minutes might make all the difference between happiness and misery for the years to come, in the poor cottage.

"She's born in the image of God. There's more than beauty . . . more than perfection in His creation. This sort of poor little creature is born to happily married mothers . . . nothing to do with sin, nothing to do with unworthiness. It's a chance, just as it was a chance, that Rachael came along that lonely road and encountered a sick, savage beast. The road at her feet at this moment is just as lonely, just as disastrous. She's going to want all the help you can give her . . . all the love."

She drew her breath in sharply and straightened up to face the task of breaking the news to the girl herself. As she reached the door to the bedroom, she looked back at him.

"You were the one, who said the body didn't matter. You said it . . . not I. You even got me round to believing that what you said might be true. Have I to convince you of your own beliefs?"

She was amazed to see him stoop his head and lay his lips against the child's cold cheek. His voice was softer than she would have thought possible.

"It was the look of the poor mite. I done wrong to forget God's mercy. She's God's Mercy in a way. Ain't she though . . . safe in His arms for ever?"

Francesca still felt dispirited the next day, when she went along to Regent House. Perhaps Rachael would forget the agony of spirit she was suffering at the moment . . . not forget it completely, but at least time would dull the edge of it. Esmond however seemed in no way able to forget the scene that had occurred in the nurse's house. The memory of it had slid down between them like a sheet of plate glass. The weeks passed slowly with over-politeness on both sides and far too many awkward little silences. The work of the practice went on inexorably and the patients never guessed that their doctors had their own personal worries and their own heartbreaks. Francesca began to persuade herself anew that she must seek a new job. She had stayed far too long in Harton. Then one evening, Mr. Caston Price, the Obstetrician from the Maternity Hospital, came out on consultation to see a Mrs. Watts and she discussed the matter with him. She had been his registrar a year before, so they

251

were well acquainted with each other, but it seemed strange to see him away from his setting in the wards and the corridors and the theatre, in the more informal background of the patient's house. They had gone down to the living-room after his examination of the patient, and when the discussion was at an end, she had asked him rather diffidently if he knew of any possible post for her. He had been studying the photographs on the mantelpiece in the restless manner, that was so characteristic of him and he spun round on her in surprise, his brows shooting up.

"I thought you were going to marry Ross? He's in deep where you're concerned . . . head over heels, as they say. Hadn't you noticed the symptoms?"

It cost her quite an effort to laugh it off. She hoped he did not recognise the false coin in her amusement, though he missed very little, as well she remembered.

"Don't you start off on that, sir. Everybody I meet these days seem determined to push me into his arms, but it's no good. He's not in search of a wife. I'm a prospective partner in the practice, but there wasn't a view to marriage."

He shifted about on his feet like a boxer

and shrugged his shoulders, possessed with the same boundless energy and zest for life, that he always had.

"So you're not in love with him after all? Is that the lie of the land?"

She evaded the answer to that.

"I'm a career woman."

He put back his head and laughed.

"A career woman? Oh, come now, Frankie. It doesn't show . . . not one damn bit."

He jingled the silver in his pocket and grinned at her reproachful look, thinking of the strange up-bringing she had had. He knew the guardian slightly . . . a chap with a bearded face like a chimpanzee. Still, he had managed to turn out a damned attractive woman and she was putting up some sort of a smoke screen about Ross.

"You know I can't get my life all cluttered up with love and marriage and babies, sir. I always intended to specialise. I only came here to help out for a few months, because Ess-mond was sick. He'd be far happier with a male assistant. . . ."

That was not what they said at the hospital, thought Caston Price, picking up the heavy obstetric bag, as if it was as light as a feather

253

and swinging it out in an arc, as he made for the door.

"So I'm to find you a job? Is that it?"

"If you hear of a vacancy . . . I'd be very grateful. . . ."

"Sounds like a good cook-general. Very well then, I'll keep you in the picture, as we say in hospital circles. Now let's go upstairs and confer with Mrs. Watts. If she gives you any more trouble, send her up to one of my sessions and we'll have her in."

Five minutes later, he was throwing the bag into the back of his car, climbing in behind the wheel, to smile at her through the open window.

"I'll keep it in mind about that job. There are plenty of openings for a good willing girl, or so they tell me. Good-bye for now . . . must be on my way . . . Ozzie Caston Price . . . the one-man emergency flying squad. . . ."

He was just as full of hustle and vitality the next morning, for all the fact that he had been up for hours in the night in the operating theatre of the General. His wife got up from the breakfast table and picked up a typed list from the sideboard.

"I've been meaning to ask you if you know Frankie Cunningham's address at Harton.

I'm getting out the invitations for the sherry party next month and I know she doesn't live at Regent House I suppose 'Harton' would find her?"

He swung his wrist over to look at his watch.

"God! That reminds me. . . ."

He was on his feet and half way to the door in a flash, answering her over his shoulder, as if it was some terrific joke.

"Leave it for a week or two . . . save you the price of a stamp. You could send one invitation and address it to Dr. and Mrs. Esmond Ross, if I play my cards right."

She followed him along to his study and found him at his desk with the phone in his hand.

"She doesn't arrive at Regent House till nine o'clock," he said in explanation. "I've got to speak to her urgently."

"But it's only eight thirty . . ." she started and he looked at her with a smile.

"Did you ever see your husband in the role of Cupid . . . standing in personally for the President of the Lonely Hearts Club?"

Of course, he was delighted at her mystification and highly amused at whatever joke he was perpetrating. She listened as he asked if he might speak to Dr. Cunningham.

"Oh, very well Connie . . . if she's not available, perhaps you'd let me speak to Dr. Ross himself."

There was a short interval in which he stood up to fidget with the pile of letters on the far side of the desk and then he settled himself down in his chair again and leaned back.

"Good morning, Esmond. I rather wanted to have a word with your young lady, but Connie tells me she hasn't arrived there yet . . . thought she had breakfast with you. Oh, well then, perhaps you'd give her a message. You know she asked me to look out for a post for her. You didn't? She has her heart set on obstetrics, you know. She asked me about it yesterday. Anyhow, the point is this . . . I've been thinking it over and I remembered a chap I met at the Royal College the other day . . . asked me if I knew of a promising female colleague for a senior registrarship. She'd have a pretty good chance of getting a junior consultant's job in a year or two. It's some new unit they're setting up in the West Country and they want a woman. This chap says good women are scarce . . . wastage in marriage and all that. . . ."

The wink he directed at Mrs. Caston Price was without shame.

"I'll give her the full details in a day or two. . . ."

He had never heard Ross's voice so miserable, as it spoke in his ear.

"She hasn't mentioned it to me."

Caston Price had got to his feet again and was leaning against the desk.

"I'll have to look up this bloke's name and address and get in touch with him, but there's no doubt he'll jump at her."

"I didn't know she wanted to leave . . . here."

There was no possible doubt that Ross was upset . . . probably thought he was far too old for the girl. And what did the President of the Lonely Hearts Club say to that, Caston Price wondered.

"I don't think she wants to leave you, old man. In fact, I know that she'd stay very happily with you for the rest of her natural life. She thinks it's time to get out. That's all."

"Time to get out?" Ross's voice echoed. "Why should she want to get out?"

"Because she's managed to fall in love with you and she's taken it into her head that you

257

don't think of her in that light. She told me only yesterday that you engaged her to help in the practice . . . not as a possible wife."

"Good Lord, Caston Price! Is this your idea of a joke? You ring up about some message I'm to give Kit and then you start. . . ."

"Ask her to marry you and see what she says to that first. You can always give her my message afterwards."

He put back the receiver before Ross could say anything and knew very well the storm of emotion he had started in the other man's heart.

"And who is this doctor in the West Country?" his wife was asking and Caston Price sat down at his desk again with a sigh and reached for the pile of letters.

"I suppose you could call him a figment of my imagination. . . ."

That afternoon, when Francesca had left the house after lunch, Esmond put through a trunk call to Murdo at Oxford, and he spoke for six minutes before he found the courage to come to the point.

"Actually, I rang about Francesca. I don't know if you'll be very angry with me, but I'm . . . I'm . . . I'm very much in love with her. I expect you'll say it's ridiculous, but for a time, I thought she was beginning to care for me too. It's the correct procedure to ask your permission to speak to her about it. You can tell me to go to hell, if you think fit."

Murdo's roar of laughter almost deafened him and he held the receiver a little away from his ear.

"The lassie's daft about you, you fool . . . has been ever since she clapped eyes on you. She's of the mind that you're the most elegant fellow she's ever met in all her born days. Ask her, my dear chap. I give you my blessing. I'll be delighted to get her off my hands."

He had hardly put down the phone, when it rang again and his face flushed a little as he heard her voice. It was the half day and she wanted to ask him to excuse her if she did not come to Regent House for dinner. Mrs. Watts was in labour at last, it seemed, and would almost certainly have her out during the night. She wanted to get to bed early to rest. He took a deep breath and knew he was losing her. In some intangible way, she was slipping out of his life for ever and he was filled with desperation.

"I'd be most obliged if you would come, Kit. I've got something to discuss with you . . . something very important."

"Now what have I done?" she asked him with a laugh. "Or have I left something undone?"

"It's nothing like that. It's about your future . . . something I discussed with your guardian today."

Now he was committed to proposing marriage to her tonight. He would tell her that he loved her and then she would go away from Harton and he would never see her any more. As with everything to do with her, he was making a mess of this, proposing to her when she was on call for a case.

"Of course, I'll come, if you wish. I've got some visits to finish and I must look in on Mrs. Watts. I'll see you at seven."

She tried to ring Murdo at the flat to find out what was going on, but the janitor answered the call and told her that Dr. Cunningham had gone out and would not be back before the evening. As she went from house to house, she wondered what the important thing was that Esmond wanted to discuss with her. She had got no nearer to the solution when she dropped in on Mrs. Watts and found her tensed up and nervy.

"When will the baby be born, Dr. Frankie? I know Mr. Caston Price said it'd come natural, but do think it's all right?"

She sat on the edge of the bed and took the girl's hand in hers.

"It's a little on the slow side. That's all. The old wives would have told you it's a lazy girl."

"That's what Mum said just now. 'You mark my words!' she said. 'That's going to be a little old lazy girl.' That's what Mum said."

"Well if this baby's as pretty as her own mother, we won't want to change her, will we? They tell me you won a beauty competition in Yarmouth last year."

She would not win it now. Her face was swollen and red, her eyes pink with weeping, her body grotesque in its shapelessness. She had even left out her dental plate with its two front teeth. It was strange how some women ceased to care for their personal appearance as pregnancy progressed. Yet some looked more attractive, as a ripe peach might look, or an animal, sleek and beautiful in fruitfulness.

Francesca went back to the nurse's house, when she had talked for a long time to Mrs. Watts. She had a leisurely bath and changed into a white backless dress, which showed up the suntan she had achieved in the perfect summer weather of the last weeks. She

261

decided that she would be different from her usual tweedy self, and take the white fur stole, that had been Murdo's Christmas gift. Perhaps if she looked more sophisticated, he would think her less of a child, than seemed to be his custom. She never failed to feel callow before his sureness and his adult quality. She had come to the conclusion that he was going to offer her a partnership. He had discussed it with Murdo and that gentleman had been mean enough not to ring and tell her about it. If that was what the important subject of discussion was, she would turn down his offer. She had made her mind up that she must leave. Perhaps she would forget him? She looked at him down the length of the dining-table later that night and knew she could never forget him. The old pain had started in the roots of her throat, as appalling as it had ever been.

He came down the room, leaning on his stick to pull out her chair, so that she could rise and go through to the sitting-room. The stole had slipped off her shoulder to the floor and he stooped and picked it up to carry it on his arm. As she sat in her customary armchair and lit the burner under the Cona, he laid it round her again and she shivered a little.

"What did you want to discuss with me, Ess-mond?"

He went over to the window and stood there, leaning on his stick, looking out into the drive.

"It's about your future here," he started and then the telephone burred outside and they sat waiting for the inevitable message of a doctor's house.

It was half a minute before Connie came in, her face anxious.

"There's an urgent message from the Grange, Dr. Frankie. Mr. Mallory rang and he says something bad's happened. He wants you to go up there right away."

"But Miss Mallory is Dr. Ross's case, Connie."

"I told him that, miss, but he says it's nothing to do with the practice. It's a private matter and it's terribly urgent and you're to go quick. If you take my advice, all the same, you'll take your medical bag. He sounded sick . . . very sick indeed."

Esmond had turned from the window and now he offered to accompany her, but she shook her head.

"I'll ring if I want you. You're tired out. I'll get back soon and we'll have that discussion and then you can get off to your bed."

The M.G. went through the drive gates far too fast as usual. He would have to speak to her about that, Esmond thought and wondered what was wrong in the Grange. It was probably some scheme of Lucien Mallory's to get her up there by herself.

"I think I'd better go after her, Connie."

"That'd be the best thing to do, sir. Mr. Lucien sounded out of his mind on the phone. We don't want her to walk in on anything bad. . . ."

She was walking in on something very bad indeed at that moment. She heard high voices as she stopped the car and walked up the front steps and as she went through the great door of the house, she looked in amazement at the scene in the hall. Ellen Ferguson was sitting on the oak chest, her cap gone and her hair all down round her face, while her husband stood by her side trying to comfort her. Lucien Mallory had his back to the door, his legs straddled apart and in his right hand, he held an envelope.

"You filthy dirty rotten bitch!" he was shouting, "Your cess pool of a mind has

264

caused enough trouble in the village, but it will cause no more."

"Ellen didn't write it," the old man quavered. "She couldn't write a thing like that, sir. She wouldn't write one of those things to Dr. Cunningham. She likes Dr. Cunningham."

Francesca took the envelope out of Lucien's hand and his face flooded with colour, as he saw her at his side.

"Thank God you've come. Perhaps you'll know what to do. Ellen must have gone off her head. She's been sending out poison pen letters. I've had one of them myself . . . and I caught her just now, with the damn thing in her hand, on the way out to post it to you."

Francesca looked down at the envelope and saw the familiar aquamarine ink, the letters that ran higgledy-piggledy, the cheap paper.

"It's no good blaming Ellen . . . no good blaming anybody. I'm glad you let me know about it, for it's a medical problem and we'd best take it more quietly."

"I'm glad you don't think I should have kept you out of it, but I thought you'd be able to talk to Ellen. . . ."

She looked at him grimly, her voice flat and lifeless.

"We'd better talk to Miss Mallory."

"You're not going to drag Aunt Charlotte into this filthy mess, are you? Have you any idea of the stuff you'll find when you open that envelope?"

"Indeed I have."

She put her arm round Ellen and helped her to her feet, guided her up the stairs.

"Come, Ellen, I know all about it. I know you've done nothing to be ashamed of. You didn't even know what was in those letters. Even if you guessed it, you couldn't know what to do. You might have come to me perhaps, but it wouldn't have made any difference in the long run."

They walked into Miss Mallory's room with Lucien still protesting and Ellen threw herself down on her knees at the bedside.

"Oh, madam, I'm sorry. Mr. Lucien found out. . . ."

Francesca laid the letter down on the counterpane and looked into the handsome old face.

"Do you remember our talk in this bedroom a few weeks ago and how you gave me your word? I'm sorry to tell you that Ellen has just been caught red-handed with this letter addressed to me. She's still your faithful servant. She hasn't said anything. . . ."

The old lady picked up the envelope and looked at it in surprise.

"It's no business of Ellen's. You did right to come to me, but you're under some apprehension, my dear. You always seem to be under some misapprehension. Last time, it was Dr. Esmond . . . or one of the last times . . . here in this very room. I told you he was in love with you and that you loved him too, and you were quite put out that I knew about it, but it was true."

Her voice rambled on unconcernedly and nobody noticed that Esmond had come in and was standing by the door.

"He never loved Sheelagh. She swept him off his feet, as she would any man. They were all anxious to take her to their beds, but he got the honour of it, and much good it did him! He knows what it is to love a woman now, because, my dear, with all your nonsense, you're a very fine woman, and he's a fine man."

She looked down at the letter and wrinkled her brow, her voice vague suddenly.

"Of course, I wrote this to you. I don't know how it came to be like the others. I'm upset that you thought I broke my word, for of course, I never did any such thing. . . ."

Her hand went to her breast and she looked up with her face contorted with pain.

"Oh, dear! I've got this knife in my chest again. It was bad this morning . . . my tablets . . . get my tablets . . . quickly, Ellen . . . Ellen . . . Ellen . . ."

She stretched her hand for the rosewood desk on her bedside table, clutched at it with such desperation that she brought it crashing to the floor and it burst open to shower its contents across the carpet . . . the cut-out words from the newspaper, the long cut-out texts from the Bible, the scissors, the gum, the notepaper, the ball-point pen. She pitched sideways out of the bed herself, before anybody could catch her and lay there on the floor in all the debris of the Poison Pen Case and in the background Lucien's voice muttered again and again "Aunt Charlotte wrote them . . . Aunt Charlotte wrote them," his face ashen with shock.

Francesca knelt down by Miss Mallory's side and took a pillow to put it under her head, thinking what a narrow margin there was between life and death . . . a long sighing breath, a screwing up of the patrician face as if farewell was a bitter thing, eyes that filled with tears.

"Get my medical bag from the car, Ferguson."

She was startled by Esmond's voice. Even as she put her hand on the silent chest, she was thinking to herself that he had been in the room and must have heard what Miss Mallory had said. She looked up at him and thought that her own face must be as white as his. Sudden death was a shocking, appalling thing that one could never accustom oneself to.

"She's gone, I'm afraid."

He bent down to murmur in her ear, that Miss Mallory had had a coronary before.

"If she had pain in her chest this morning, she probably had it then and this was terminal . . . inevitable . . . a mercy really. She never took kindly to being an invalid."

They lifted her back to the bed, closed her eye-lids, pulled the sheet over her face and Lucien Mallory's hands were shaking as if he had a fever.

"Will there have to be an inquest . . . an inquiry?"

Esmond shook his head.

"Of course not. I've been attending her for

many years and I saw her only yesterday. There'll be no unpleasantness. I suggest that the fire is the place of choice for that litter from the desk. What's happened need go no further than the four walls of this room."

It seemed a long time before they were out in the drive again and Francesca took in a deep breath of the fresh evening air, feeling relief at being out of the drama of the silent room. She had picked up the letter, that had been the beginning of the whole disastrous affair and had thrust it into her pocket. It crackled against her side as Esmond opened the door of the M.G. and she got in behind the wheel.

"I seem to have blocked your way with my car," he said. "I'll go on ahead and you can follow me up."

She drove round the bend in the avenue, where she was out of sight of the house and pulled the car to a halt, before she took out the letter. It seemed very peaceful under the trees in the filtered light, with only the conversation of the rooks to break the stillness, as she slid her thumb under the flap of the envelope and took out the sheet of notepaper.

"Dear Miss Francesca,

I am writing this letter to beg you to believe what I told you the first day I met you. Esmond Ross loves you very dearly, but he had confided in me, that you do not care for him. I know this is not true, having seen you fly to his defence on that memorable occasion. Since then, I have watched you together and seen your face, when you look at him. Take the advice of an old, old lady, who let happiness pass her by. Don't let the same fate happen to you. Marry him, my dear child and may God bless you. . . ."

It was the same as all the other letters had been with the cut out print and the scrawled childish writing. She wondered what had induced Charlotte Mallory to send her such a harmless letter under such a wicked guise. She was unbalanced, of course. It just proved that she was not responsible for all the pain she had caused. At first, she had been angry that Esmond had taken a woman assistant and had used the letters as an attempt to make her leave the village. Then she had mistaken Esmond's feelings for her. Her face burned as she thought of the conversations that must have passed on his visits to the house. Miss

Mallory would have spoken her mind in her forthright fashion. She started the car again and halted as she reached the main road. She was glad that the letter was safely back in her pocket, as Sergeant Bullen came along on his bicycle and stopped beside her, with one hand on the windscreen.

"So Miss Mallory's had a heart attack?" he said and she looked up at him grimly.

"You've had your spies on the alert this evening, Sergeant."

"Dr. Ross told me just now, says it's all plain sailing and he can issue the certificate. Mr. Lucien will come into it all now, I suppose, and that'll suit him down to the ground."

He sighed and raised his eyes to the green branches of the elms against the sky.

"Bear in mind the advice I gave you, Doctor . . . about the worthy gentleman."

"I'll bear it in mind."

She looked down at the steering wheel and smiled.

"I've been wanting a word with you, Sergeant. I've got something to tell you. I promised to come to Inspector Taylor and yourself one day, didn't I, and tell you that there'd be no more poison pen letters? I can do it now. There'll be no more of them."

"So the cork worked, Dr. Frankie?"

She thought how true that was, for the last letter had not been written by any poison pen. She looked up and met his eyes at last, thought how shrewd he was and how full of kindness and integrity.

"It worked. The dyke held, by God's mercy."

"And will continue to hold?"

"And will continue to hold and that's an end to it . . . an end to my confidences too, for I'll tell you no more about it, even if you cross-examine me all night. . . ."

Esmond was waiting for her at the gate of Regent House.

"Where on earth have you been? Did Mallory come after you?"

His voice was irritable and he grumbled at her all the way into the sitting-room, where he put a glass of sherry into her hands.

"Now you'd better begin at the beginning and tell me all about this business of Charlotte Mallory and the anonymous letters. It was she you suspected, I suppose, but you failed to put a stop to them."

She had no intention of denying that. She told him what had happened in her interview with the old lady and when she had finished, he scolded her for trying to deal with the problem herself.

"At the very least, you should have confided in me. Miss Mallory was my patient, after all, not yours. . . ."

He was put out with her about the whole affair, but she knew that she must correct any impression he might have picked up, when he walked into Miss Mallory's room an hour before.

"There was one other thing, Ess-mond. I don't know when you came into the room tonight . . . Miss Mallory's room, I mean. . . ."

He was standing at the drinks cabinet and he poured three fingers of scotch into a big crystal tumbler.

"About half a minute after yourself, I imagine," he said dryly.

She tried to will the blood not to flow into her cheeks and knew she came short of success.

"You heard all that rot about you and me then. I was hoping you hadn't. Don't feel awkward about it. I don't."

And that was a fine lie, she thought.

"She got that bee in her bonnet about your being in love and it was all her usual wandering nonsense . . . a proof, really, how unstable she was mentally. I told her the first day I met her that I'd be far more likely to marry Simon, the cat, than marry you."

She tried to smile at him but made a poor job of it and then she staggered awkwardly and slowly on with her explanation.

"No, I didn't say that to her. I said it to Lucien, just afterwards. He was on about the same topic, after I almost ran him down in the drive. I told him to have a sense of proportion and not to talk foolishness. . . ."

He raised his glass to his lips and drank a good half of the whisky in one gulp and she thought it time to make a joke to try to ease the tension that was building up in the room. She managed to inject a schoolboy camaraderie into the words and knew she sounded impertinent and that it made him angrier than ever.

"I'd go easy on that Glen Livet, if I were you. I'm likely to want an anaesthetic for Mother Watts at any moment now. I don't want to find you drunk and disorderly."

He put down the glass abruptly and came across the room to take hers out of her hand, to set it on the mantelpiece.

"You told Mallory that you'd rather marry

Simon than marry me?" he demanded furiously, and she looked up into his angry face.

"Your predicate is wrong."

He took her shoulders between his two hands and shook her sharply, so that her hair fell across her forehead.

"*Vicisti* and boundless seas and St. Catherine's erudition and corrections in grammar! You told Mallory that?"

"You're hurting me, Ess-mond."

He let her go and wheeled away towards the door. The stick in his hand had bruised her shoulder and she rubbed it ruefully.

"I don't know why you're so angry. Truly I don't. I told him that I'd be far more likely to marry Simon. That was all. My likes and dislikes didn't come into it."

He had turned with one hand on the door knob and was frowning back at her, thinking against his will that he had never seen her look more lovely than she did at that moment, her shoulder clasped in her hand and the long white stole trailing to the floor.

"May I have some explanation of what you meant, or is it too much trouble?"

"Oh dear!" she murmured and sat down suddenly, her elbows on her knees and her forehead in her hands.

276

"Well?"

"Miss Mallory said I should marry you and then I met Lucien in the drive . . . that first day. He said I'd marry you one day. It was all terribly silly . . . not the least bit serious. I said that about Simmy, because I knew the idea was ridiculous. I knew what you felt for me. I know what you feel for me now, come to that. You didn't want me at first . . . not for an assistant. Then, when I came, you were sorry for me, because I had no parents and Murdo had obviously told you that I had had. . . ."

She came to a halt and sat silently and miserably for a moment. Then she saw his shoes appear in her line of vision and knew that he was standing over her, looking down on her bent head.

"Murdo had told me what?"

"About my 'vaccination' against love. I told you about it myself later anyhow, but you knew it that first night. You took me in because you're a kind man. I was a stray dog and you couldn't help feeling sorry for me. Then after a bit, you thought I was amusing . . . like a kitten. You know you said that yourself. I made silly jokes and laughed far too much and you were so very serious. Yet you liked the nonsense . . . in a kind of way. Perhaps I helped with the practice too. I was around like a dog, to carry your slippers to the fire and lay my head on your knee."

He sat down on the arm of her chair and put the stole back round her shoulders, left his arm around her, stroking her shoulder with his finger.

"Well?"

"That's all there is to it. These people were foolish. You don't fall in love with every stray cur, that carries your slippers. . . ."

His fingers still soothed away the hurt from her shoulder and all his anger was gone.

"Besides which," he put in. "You told me very firmly that you could never fall in love again."

"Oh, that was changed. . . ."

It was out before she could stop herself. She jumped to her feet and looked down at him, her face dismayed. Then she went off across the room like a rabbit.

"Francesca, come here. If you don't come back this instant, I'll follow you and bring you back."

She tore the door open and found Connie on the threshold.

"Dr. Frankie! Nurse rang just now and

278

you're wanted at Mrs. Watts. She says you're to be sure to change out of that dress. She's brought down your ski suit. It's all ready in the surgery.

Francesca turned her head to mutter an excuse to Esmond and ran down the hall into her consulting-room. She was stepping into her ski pants, when Connie came in to collect the midwifery kit.

"Dr. Esmond told me to put the bags in his car. He'll take you down to the case himself."

She found him standing at the front door, awaiting her. Connie was fussing along at her heels with the anaesthetic case in her hand, beaming all over her face.

"I was just thinking that Dr. Frankie looks very same as the first night she stepped into this hall . . . suntan and all. It's like as if the time has moved back."

He looked at her gravely.

"There's a subtle difference that you wouldn't know about yet, Connie. Perhaps I'll wake you up and tell you all about it, when I get back."

He turned the car out into the main road and Francesca glanced at him briefly.

"It's good of you to drive me down, Essmond."

He lifted one eyebrow at her and smiled.

"Dogs aren't allowed out alone after sunset without their collars. Don't you know that?"

So he was joking about it now? She had never felt less like joking in her life. It was a good thing that the Watt's house was so close. She jumped out of the car with more speed than grace and ran in through the front door and up the stairs.

"There's no hurry, Dr. Frankie," Nurse Roberts told her as she came into the room. "You can wash up in your own good time. We're getting on famously here."

Watts was bringing the cases up to the bedroom. She went to sit on the edge of the bed and talk to Mrs. Watts, routine stuff, that seemed to come out of her mouth automatically. She had no idea what she was talking about, or so it seemed, but Nurse Roberts was laughing, so presumably it must have been something funny, she thought to herself, as she donned her gown and mask. She felt relieved that Esmond had not followed her upstairs. Perhaps he had gone back to Regent House. She went out to the bathroom with a sigh of relief, and then quite suddenly, he appeared at her shoulder, watching her reflection in the glass over the basin.

"You know you were talking nonsense to me just now, don't you, Kit?"

She scrubbed her nails with the small brush, bending her head down, as if the task required fierce concentration. Then she washed her hands and arms, lathering them with soap and rinsing them again and again. He was very amused about something, but she was so confused in her mind, that all she could think of was that his eyebrows were just like a devil's eyebrows, coming up to angle out like they did. That was what she had thought the first night she saw him.

"It wasn't nonsense. It was my interpretation of the case in hand," she muttered gruffly after a while, and still he smiled at her.

It was a relief when Nurse Roberts came in to talk to them for a moment and soon she was holding the door open for Francesca to return to the bedroom.

"Mr. Caston Price telephoned after you went down to the surgery this evening, Dr. Frankie," she said, as they reached the bedside. "He wanted to speak to you particularly, asked if you'd had a message from

Dr. Ross. Apparently he has some news for you . . . about a new job."

She looked enquiringly at Esmond and he muttered rather awkwardly that he had forgotten all about it, but Nurse Roberts filled in the details.

"There's a colleague of Mr. Caston Price's, who wants a senior registrar. Mr. Caston Price thought you might consider it, unless you had something else in mind. He was laughing about it, but I couldn't, for the life of me, see what he thought was funny. They want a woman doctor. He said you'd get the job for sure with his backing. It's in the West Country some place . . . a lovely district. It's vacant shortly."

"Oh, you're not going, Dr. Frankie," moaned Mrs. Watts from the bed. "Please don't leave me."

"I'm not going this minute at any rate. I don't know about later. One shouldn't stay too long in one place. . . ."

Esmond had left the room, as she spoke and the nurse was whisking the covers from the instrument table.

"You ask Mrs. Watts here about staying too long in one place, Dr. Frankie. Her Grandpa Jordan Black, had an unfortunate experience, that just about proves your point."

The patient was lifting her flushed face from the pillow.

"Goo you on, Nurse, you mean the story about the poor old chap. You want I'll tell that?"

She stopped up short and grabbed for the mask of the anaesthetic machine and Francesca tried to force her own thoughts back to the bedroom and the case in hand.

"Take three breaths, Mrs. Watts. Now, here's the fourth. Don't let it go. We've shown you how to do it. There! That's very good indeed."

The hot face appeared from the mask again to look up in hers.

"Anybody in the village would tell you that one, Dr. Frankie. He were a rare one for the beer and he were getting on, must have been eighty-four and it were his birthday, so he went down the 'Black Horse' to celebrate. . . ."

Francesca kept her eyes on the door of the room nervously and hoped that her chief would not come in again, and Mrs. Watts's story ran in the background of her mind.

"In those days, there were a stream there . . . covered in now, but it's still called Water

Lane. You might ha' wondered why. My grandpa had eight pints of beer aboard that night, seeing it were his birthday and on the way home, up Water Lane, he had to stop in the dark . . . you know why. Course, he could hear the stream a-running and he thought it were . . . Oh, God, here's another pain. . . ."

Francesca wondered if the story would ever get told, but the last instalment was coming up now.

"He stood there for an hour . . . honest he did, Dr Frankie. He was waiting for the stream to stop and my Gran had to goo out and fetch him home in the finish. . . ."

"Well, Mrs. Watts is in the finish herself this minute," Nurse Roberts laughed and Francesca wondered if her anaesthetist had taken himself home.

"I'll report you to the Shire Hall for encouraging such stories over the birth of a baby, Robbie," she said and Esmond came back into the room as the nurse spoke.

"You may as well laugh as cry, but I'm surprised you hadn't heard the tale before."

"What tale, Kit?" Esmond asked and she pretended she was very engrossed with her patient and promised him rather absent-mindedly that she would tell him later.

"I want a word with you anyhow, as soon as we're through here," he told her as he sat down to pick up the anaesthetic mask.

He looked at her to his heart's content, but she would not meet his eyes. Her laughter was hollow too and he recognised it as whistling in the dark. How could she have thought herself of so little importance to him, he wondered, and cursed the slowness of midwifery.

The baby was almost born now, he saw, and she had started talking almost to herself, which was a habit of hers on such occasions. For the moment, she had no consciousness of any other person or thing, but the work in hand.

"It's coming now . . . very nice relaxation. There we are! It's a bruiser too. If it's a girl, she's got the face of a prize fighter . . . rather unfortunate, with a beauty queen as a mother. Such shoulders . . . this is where one tells oneself that there's no cause for panic. No . . . cause . . . for . . . panic . . . no . . . hurry . . . in the world. Why does it always feel so damned urgent? There we are . . . a boy too."

She gave a long sigh of relief, all her tension gone in a flash and smiled at them.

"It's ten pounds at a guess, but there's a bad tear. We'll be here all night and I'll be glad of such an expert anaesthetist."

She separated the baby from its mother and passed it to the nurse.

"Robbie, will you tell Mr. Watts the good news? He's worried out of his wits. Then be an angel and let's have that reading lamp round this side of the bed. I'll want some good light."

There was the same impression that she spoke to herself as she picked up the needle holder.

"I often wonder how I can be so very fond of the First Gentleman . . . fonder of him than I'd be of any mother, without a cord to join us . . . a kind of metaphysical cord, I suppose . . . more enduring than flesh and blood."

Her eyes never lifted from the site of operation, as she went on.

"He found me crying in bed one night . . . after my parents were gone. I was a bit over ten years of age and I had managed to wait till I was in bed and the lights were out. Murdo had kissed me and tucked me up, but he came back . . . put out a hand in the dark to feel my face. He had the kindness not to shame me by turning on the light. I don't know why he came back, but he knew. I had managed not to make a noise, so it wasn't that. . . ."

"So?"

"It must have been nine or ten o'clock, but he made up a fire in the grate . . . at no small danger to the flat too, for he transferred it from the study fire on a shovel. Then he turned on the light . . . only then. He brought in a bottle of whisky for himself and a syphon of soda . . . and lemon squash for me. He propped me up in wonderful comfort . . . got out a lovely old edition of David Copperfield. He told me that it was better than sleeping any day, to have an assignation with a beautiful lady at midnight. Then he turned his back on me and said it was no disgrace to be weeping, if your heart was broken. I remember he pointed out that David Copperfield had had his heart broken, but he'd found happiness in the end . . . and so should I. Then he grinned at me and told me his feelings would not be hurt if I 'dropped off' during the reading. . . ."

She threw the needleholder into a basin with a clatter and stretched her arms above her head, yawned.

"That's that then."

Nurse Roberts bustled across to untie the tapes at the back of her gown.

"I'll finish up here and take the kit home with me. Away home to your bed, Dr. Frankie, before you fall asleep. . . ."

She walked before him down the stairs and got into the car and his heart had started to beat in great pounding strokes, as he walked round the bonnet of the car to get in beside her. There was no putting it off any longer, he thought, as he started the engine and drove off along the road.

"I'll turn here."

He ran the nose of the car into a deserted unmade roadway, went on for twenty yards, stopped, put out the lights, switched off the engine.

"So you've given me a pretty standard of perfection to measure up to, haven't you?"

"Why have you stopped? Is anything the matter?"

It was a clear moonlight night and he could see her face distinctly, as his eyes grew accustomed to the darkness.

"I wanted to ask you a question, Kit . . . an important question . . . important to me, that is. Do you think you could ever bring yourself . . . perhaps in a little while, if not now, do you think you could do me the honour . . . of marrying me?"

The words were out, fallen from his dry mouth into the stillness of the night and the effect on her was electric. She had been lying back on her seat and she sat bolt upright, her eyes wide, her face startled.

"What did you say?" she demanded.

"I asked you if you'd do me the honour of becoming my wife. Of course, I quite understand, that at a very early age, you dedicated yourself to celibacy . . . and to the Royal Candian Mounted Police and that later on you got mixed up with medicine . . . and I also realise that, up to now, you haven't been available as an ordinary wife, but do you think you could become a very extraordinary one, my darling, for you're a very extraordinary person?"

She still looked at him increduously.

"*Me* marry *you* . . . *me* marry *you*. You really don't mean what you're saying. I knew you drank that whisky far too fast, but that anaesthetic was beautifully given. . . ."

"Oh, Kit, you're hopeless."

He was laughing now as she had never heard him laugh.

"You love me, Kit. I can see that you do."

"Of course I love you," she complained in an aggrieved voice. "I just didn't think that you thought of me like that. I told you. . . ."

"We've been through all that, my faithful hound. Come here for a moment. You shouldn't be out without your collar at this hour of the night."

He put an arm round her to draw her head down on his shoulder and felt her face against his neck. He kissed her hand and slid his signet ring down over her finger, whispering at her ear.

"Will that do for a collar tonight? We'll see about something far more splendid in a day or two."

He was kissing her now, gently and lingering.

"I don't know about the lead. One has to fashion a bond, as Murdo did. I shall never match up to the First Gentleman, shall I?"

Her voice was a whisper against his mouth.

"The First Gentleman is dead. Long live the First Gentleman! He told me it would happen, just as it's happened. I don't love him any the less . . . rather more perhaps . . . and it's not necessary to forge any bond between us, for it's forged already. I tried to get away and it held me fast. It was made up

290

of so many strange and wonderful things. . . ."

"Wonderful?" he echoed her whisper.

"The way you held my hand at Wentbridge Station and forgot to let it go . . . the way I seemed to be coming home, though I had never been in Harton before . . . the elegance of Your Majesty . . . your distinguished look . . . the two wings of white in your dark hair . . . the gravity of your eyes . . . the depth in them . . . the way you scolded me that night, but only because you loved me . . . the way you laughed at all my poor jokes, and tried to look at life another way, just to oblige me . . . the humility of your love, non-demanding and very patient. I could go on with this list of things all night, Ess-mond."

"You may if you like," he laughed. "I've no intention of taking you home for a very long time."

He kissed the edge of her eyebrow and came by pleasant stages back to her mouth again. Then he raised his head.

"What was that joke you and Nurse Roberts were laughing at?"

"Joke?"

"Just before the baby was born; you said you were going away from me and I went out to the car to sulk. I admit it. When I came back, you were all laughing, even poor Mrs. Watts, who wasn't in a very happy state at that moment. What was it all about?"

She put back her head and began to laugh.

"It was about Grandfather Black, Essmond, but I don't think it's very suitable for this particular moment of our lives."

"Tell me."

"That's medicine all over," she grumbled. "If we weren't doctors, you'd take my hand and whisper in my ear. You'd say . . .

"How sweet the moonlight sleeps upon this
      bank!
Here will we sit and let the sounds of music
Creep in our ears; soft stillness and the night
Become the touches of sweet harmony . . .
Look how the floor of heaven
Is thick inlaid with patines of bright
      gold. . . ."

She settled herself more comfortably in his arms and smiled.

"But being doctors, as I've just said, I must give you the past history of Grandfather Black, aged eighty-four . . . and on your own head be it! Don't tell me afterwards that you didn't insist on it."

It was obvious to Simon that they had forgotten all about him. It was equally obvious that there was no chance of their going home for hours yet. He showed his pink tongue in a prodigious yawn and curled himself up into a ball on his blue cushion in the back window, with a sigh of resignation.

THE END

P   EL   Two